SNIPER
COUNTER SNIPER

A GUIDE FOR
SPECIAL RESPONSE TEAMS

by

MARK V. LONSDALE

S.T.T.U.

SPECIALIZED TACTICAL
TRAINING UNIT

DISCLAIMER

The author, S.T.T.U. and those that contributed to this book take no responsibility for the use or misuse of the material herein.

SNIPER/COUNTER SNIPER was written as a guide to qualified and experienced law enforcement personnel, with no intention of contradicting their current agencies' policies.

No moral or legal conclusions should be drawn from any of the following material. We have tried to present the mechanics of sniper deployment, leaving legal and policy decisions to the individual agencies concerned.

All training should be under the control of qualified instructors and all operations under the control of qualified commanders.

SNIPER/COUNTER SNIPER

First Printing August 1986
Second Printing 1987
Third Printing December 1990
Fourth Printing 1993

Copyright © 1987/1993 by Mark V. Lonsdale
Los Angeles, California 90049

ISBN 0-939-235-00-5

Library of Congress Catalog Card Number 86-061461

PRINTED IN THE UNITED STATES OF AMERICA

DEDICATION

To the man who first told me, **"ACCURACY IS THE PRODUCT OF UNIFORMITY,"** Ian Campbell. A fine shot and a true gentleman who encouraged a thirteen-year-old lad to take his shooting seriously. And to my father for years of encouragement and support.

Last but not least, to "the men in the arena."

ACKNOWLEDGEMENTS

SNIPER/COUNTER SNIPER could not have been written without a great deal of assistance from many people over the years. Special thanks go to the following people:

Karen K. Lewis for the hours of photography, typing and proofing
Bill Hahn for the excellent illustrations and cartoons
Kathy Erickson for art work
Ron Gearhart (LESA), Larry Albach and Dan Baxter for years of expertise and assistance
Tom Riley for his input on the physical conditioning of special teams
Roger Green and the Green Canyon Combat Range
Ed Johnson for camera work
John Satterwhite of Heckler & Koch
Robbie Barrkman of ROBAR
All the companies and individuals that have supplied data and equipment over the years, too numerous to name.

With my deepest thanks, "keep up the good work."

ABOUT THE AUTHOR

Mark Lonsdale is the Founder and Director of S.T.T.U., an FBI certified Police Firearms Instructor and an NRA Rifle/Pistol Instructor.

He is also an advisor/instructor in Police /SWAT weapons and tactics, Military small unit operations and domestic or international Security problems. In the last ten years he has trained or advised members of at least forty agencies with a law enforcement/special response capability, in several different countries.

The author is an internationally recognized shooter with successes in combat pistol, rifle and shotgun competitions along with precision and sniper rifle matches. His competitive shooting began with center-fire rifle matches at the age of thirteen and continued through his military service, trying several different disciplines, to this day.

In his earlier years, prior to military service, he was a very successful Black Belt in judo competing in three World Championships while training and instructing in several countries. Then, after five years as a commercial deep sea diver he returned to the world of tactical weapons training and began developing some of the most progressive training methods in the U.S. today.

AUTHOR'S NOTE

It is very difficult to write a training manual without mentioning the manufacturers of certain weapons and pieces of equipment. It is not my intention to say that these are the only or the best makers of this type of equipment, but they are ones that we have had experience with and have found to be of exceptionally high quality.

S.T.T.U. is a training and research group with no interest in promotion or marketing of any product and the prices used in this book are approximations, subject to change and included for agency budgeting purposes only.

Since we are continually testing related equipment, and will be updating this book periodically, if you believe you have a good product, send us a sample for testing. Bear in mind that we test and evaluate under very rigorous and realistic conditions, we take no responsibility for products that do not meet the very demanding standards of this type of work.

Likewise, if in your experience you see areas lacking in this book I would like to hear about them. My aim is to produce a text that will be of considerable value to all personnel, whether military or law enforcement, who have to go out there on the sharp end to protect our rights and freedoms.

S.T.T.U.
P.O. BOX 491261
LOS ANGELES
CA 90049
U.S.A.

INTRODUCTION

SNIPER/COUNTER SNIPER began as the in-house training notes for the **S.T.T.U. Sniper Program,** but over the years we have been encouraged to make our experience available to all agencies with a sniper capability.

No book can ever replace experience, hands-on training and good instruction but we hope that this book will fill the need for a basic text on all aspects of the sniper/counter-sniper role in a law enforcement application.

The term "sniper" has been erroneously used to describe various demented individuals who have decided to start shooting, randomly, into crowds of innocent people. The Texas Tower incident of the late sixties is a prime example. The position of sniper, in the military, is one reserved for an elite group of very skilled and highly trained individuals. For this reason, throughout this book, we will refer to the rifle marksman as a **"Sniper,"** for it is indeed a title to be proud of.

The best way to neutralize a hostile sniper is with another, more skilled sniper of your own. This is where we derive the term Sniper/Counter Sniper.

The book is aimed at Police Marksmen, SWAT and Military Snipers required to work in an urban environment. S.T.T.U. has taken a simple, common-sense approach to this subject keeping in mind that many agencies must work on a limited budget.

SNIPER/COUNTER SNIPER will also be of tremendous help to administrators and instructors required to equip and train agency sniper teams.

The days of a patrol officer with his deer rifle have passed, because of a combination of liability suits and more sophisticated criminals and terrorists. But at the same time we do not need the high-dollar, Starwars approach of some groups.

The emphasis in **SNIPER/COUNTER SNIPER** is on well selected men, good, simple equipment and sound tactics.

F.B.I. statistics tell us that training and equipment should be geared for medium to close range shots, not the 1000-yard capability that the military sniper requires in a war zone.

The law enforcement sniper is required to: positively identify his target; contend with possible bystanders, hostages or team members within close proximity to the target; operate under all light and weather conditions; maintain his position for many hours, then make the shot on command; then, based on his training and experience, stand up before a board of inquiry or court and justify his actions.

For these reasons, and many others, the time and energy put into sniper training will be far disproportionate to the time actually served in this role.

CONTENTS

PART III
OPERATIONS

PART I

PREPARATION AND PLANNING

I
ROLE OF THE SNIPER

The sniper is a skilled specialist and an essential part of a tactical element. His skills must be utilized carefully and held in reserve. All too often the sniper is incorrectly deployed, then when needed is found doing crowd or traffic control on the perimeter of an operation.

The sniper's role is:

- To gain the high ground, observe and report. Supply the team with important intelligence from a safe distance: type of structure, doors, windows; any suspect movement; possible approach routes for the entry team.
- To cover the approach and movement of an assault team. Supply cover fire when necessary.
- To neutralize a dangerous suspect when so ordered.
- To neutralize a suspect vehicle.
- To provide diversionary fire for hostage rescue.

Do not lose sight of the sniper's primary role, to **COMMUNICATE AND ENGAGE PRE-SELECTED TARGETS.** He should be held under strict control and not permitted to shoot randomly.

ROLE OF SNIPER OBSERVER

In all reality the SO should be a fully qualified #2 sniper. He may have to exchange positions with the primary sniper as often as every **15 minutes** on an operation. Looking through a 10X scope continually is very fatiguing and can cause blurred vision and headaches.

The #2 sniper's additional duties would be to:

- Assist sniper with equipment
- Observe suspect location
- Handle communications
- Relieve sniper on prolonged operations
- Add firepower
- Call shots for sniper
- Supply security for sniper

Probably the most important job of the sniper/observer is to handle the communications for the primary sniper and maintain the **operational log.** This log is a detailed record of all radio traffic, intelligence information, fire control status and fire orders. The log may become an important legal document in the case of a sniper-involved shooting, so time, date and record all details.

Even though sniper #1 and sniper #2 may exchange positions they should **never exchange weapons.** No man should be expected to make a critical shot with a weapon that is zeroed for another—one more reason the sniper/observer should be a qualified and fully equipped sniper.

U.S. Marine snipers training with the M40A1.
Note Eagle drag bag used as a support.

2
SNIPER SELECTION

First and foremost the sniper or sniper candidate must be a volunteer. But, just wanting to be a sniper is not enough.

Look for men with **proven rifle shooting ability** either from the military or civilian competition. This should bring with it a working knowledge of ballistics as well.

This person should have extensive law enforcement experience with a thorough understanding of all agency policies with regard to use of deadly force.

He should be mature, calm, patient and **emotionally stable,** a **non-smoker** and preferably a non- or light drinker.

Look for a man who is physically fit and capable of climbing with heavy loads. This fitness will also help control his breathing while shooting. **Good health** means good reflexes, better muscle control and greater stamina.

Perfect eyesight is essential. Lost or broken glasses would render him useless and the glass could cause reflection to give away his location.

The man should be highly **motivated** with an eagerness to train and perfect his skills.

The sniper should be of **above average** intelligence with an ability to communicate clearly and accurately on the radio. He will need to understand ballistics, optics, communications, navigation and intelligence gathering.

Another useful skill to test for is **powers of observation.** Some people are just naturally more observant than others and will see and report details more accurately. This is also a skill that can be taught and trained. Show a candidate pictures of various situations, for a short period of time (15-20 secs.). Then ask him to describe the people in the picture, their location, type of dress, possible weapons, etc. The FBI is working in this area and developing some useful methods.

Do not be surprised if your sniper is the quiet "loner" type of person. This is a very common trait among good riflemen. He will, however, be quite proud of a good group or exceptional shot during training.

PROBATION

A sniper candidate should go through an extensive probationary period where he is regularly tested and evaluated by senior snipers and instructors.

His shooting scores must show a high degree of skill but above all must be **consistent.** "Good days and bad days" are not acceptable. The team must also develop confidence in his ability to shoot **past** them without danger. A new sniper should be watched carefully on his first few call-outs.

Not everyone is suited to sniper work. Be hard and critical in your evaluations and encourage the candidate to be **honest** with himself. If he can't do that one inch group, the consistent 100-yard head shot or the consistent 300-yard chest shot, reassign him.

If you do find a potentially good rifleman be sure to give him the **time** and **ammo** to perfect his skills.

SNIPER/OBSERVER

We would like to get away from this sniper/observer concept and encourage agencies to change to a #1 and #2 sniper system.

The sniper/observer should be a **qualified sniper** or sniper trainee. Be sure that he is not too talkative or has other habits that may distract or annoy the sniper. They will be spending many hours together in training and on operations, so should be able to function as an efficient team.

Mauser 66-SP

Dragunov S.V.D. 7.62x54R

French F1 used by GIGN

4

3
SNIPER RIFLE SELECTION

In this book we will often refer to the rifle as a weapons system because a good sniper requires more than just a **rifle.** It is the bringing together of barrel, stock and action with scope, sling, bi-pod and ammunition to form a very accurate **shooting system.**

One only has to look at the various counter-terrorist teams around the globe to realize that there is more than just one sniper weapons system available. France's **GIGN** use the F1 in 7.5mm and 7.62mm, the **USMC** the M40A1, **GSG9** the Mauser 66 and H&K PSG-1, **Israel** the Galil, **Commonwealth** units the Parker Hale, New Zealand Police **AOS/ATS** the .222 Sako, **Soviet** Bloc the SVD Dragunov, **US Army** the M21. The British **SAS** at one time had four rifles, a 22/250 with day scope and one with night scope plus a 7.62 NATO with a day scope and one with a night scope. **LAPD** adopted the H&K G3SG-1 for its rapid follow-up shots capability. The SLA incident and the Olympic Games may have influenced that decision. LA Sheriffs **SEB** also has the G3SG-1, but along with **LAPD,** have maintained their Remington 700s. Other agencies in the U.S. use modified Remington 700s, Winchester 70s and Ruger 77s, with Steyr SSG, McMillans and H&K PSG-1 becoming very popular.

We have seen every caliber utilized from .222 to .50cal with .308 Winchester being the most popular and the most practical.

What we must now establish is what is the most suited to law enforcement application in the United States.

Acceptable accuracy with reasonable cost. It is easy to spend three to six thousand dollars looking for that ultimate rifle that will hold a one-inch group at 300 yards when all we realistically need is **minute of angle,** one inch at 100 yards for closer to eight hundred dollars.

If you have the budget, by all means use it, but in most cases you will have to fight for every penny.

A group like the **FBI Hostage Rescue Team** or **DELTA** is justified in spending considerably more on their weapons since their role could involve long-range airport/aircraft counter-hijack situations or organized terrorist groups where firepower becomes a consideration.

The sniper rifle is not a general issue weapon, it is a precision instrument that should be **assigned to one man.** The rifle should be able to consistently make an accurate **COLD SHOT** under any environmental conditions.

COLD SHOT CONCEPT

The snipers' role will generally revolve around making **one accurate shot** from a cold weapon. There is no time for zeroing, sight adjustment or a second shot. If the weapons system was zeroed on a hot day at the range, the shot placement should not change during a cold, evening call-out and vice versa. During a string of fire on the range the zero should not change as the barrel of the weapon heats up.

From a clean, dry barrel, with the same high quality ammunition, there should be virtually no deviation from zero each time the weapon is taken out for training or operations.

Now this is good in theory but there will be slight deviations under various conditions. It is essential that the sniper has shot his weapon under **all conditions** and **logged the results,** so that he can now make the required compensations.

BASIC REQUIREMENTS FOR A SNIPER WEAPON

CALIBER

Although the lighter calibers of .222, .223, .243 and 22/250 have been popular in many areas because of their lack of over-penetration, mild recoil and flat trajectory, **.308Win (7.62NATO)** is still the most practical for its stopping power, long-range stability and penetration of windows and walls.

Some agencies have even tested .375 H&H, .300 WinMag and .50cal for extreme range and penetration, but this is not necessary when working in a relatively **short range** urban environment.

With any caliber, shot placement is the most critical factor so we will not dwell on a topic that has filled more books and resulted in more arguments than any other subject in the shooting world.

Sufficient to say that **.308Win** has proven itself for many years with every military unit in the free world, the **USMC** and **US Army** Sniper teams, in international competition whether it be NRA Full-bore, Bench Rest, Metallic Silhouette or Sporting Rifle.

Lastly, and probably most important, .308Win is the **only** commercially made **MATCH** grade ammo available.

THE RIFLE

The rifle should have:
- Heavy barrel, for stability, rigidity, heat transfer and accuracy.
- Stable stock, sealed or fiberglass so as to be unaffected by temperature or humidity changes.
- Magazine of at least 3 or 4 rounds for follow-up shots.
- Light, crisp trigger, 2-3 lbs.
- Rubber butt pad, not to absorb recoil but to prevent slippage on the shoulder.
- Good scope, for target identification and precise shot placement.
- Sling, for carrying and stable shooting.
- Rail and hand stop, for good sling shooting.
- Bi-pod, a tremendous aid to stability and accuracy for many shooters.

4
SNIPER RIFLES

There are many companies that manufacture rifles specifically for sniper application and have some nice features if your agency can afford them. The average small police department may not need the expense of one of these weapons, but neither can they afford the **liability** of issuing a SWAT sniper a **sub-standard** weapon that may result in a **wrongful** shooting.

STEYR SSG — One of the best out of the box, **bolt action,** sniper rifles. Synthetic (Cycolac) stock, rotary magazine in .243 or .308. The newer model, P-II, has the heavier barrel, adjustable rail under the fore-end and enlarged bolt handle.

One feature of this rifle worth comment is the optional double triggers. The way this works is by pulling, or setting, the rear trigger; you can reduce the trigger pull on the front trigger from a few pounds to mere ounces. The **slightest touch** will then cause the weapon to fire. Now this is all well and good on a target/competition rifle but not on a sniper weapon where a person's life or the rescue team's security may be at stake. In a high stress situation the trigger release must be a **positive action** on the part of the sniper, not a slight accident or premature discharge.

If you already have an **SSG** with double triggers we suggest you use it without setting the rear trigger, but if you are in the market for a new one, order it with the **single trigger.**

Steyr SSG with 6.5x-20x Leupold scope

H&K G3SG-1 — A good selection where **firepower** is more critical than super accuracy.

Equipped with a 1.5X-6X scope, 20 round magazines, sling and bipod, it is a very versatile unit but will not shoot the one-inch group expected of most sniper weapons.

H&K G3SG1 with 1.5x-6x sniper scope

H&K PSG-1 — Probably the **ultimate semi-automatic sniper system** on the market in the United States today. Comes with special heavy barrel, 6X bullet drop compensating scope, welded mounts, fully adjustable stock and grip, separate tri-pod, robust case and accessories. Many snipers prefer the semi-automatic capability for engaging multiple targets and not having to lift the head or lose sight picture to operate the bolt.

Author's note: We approached the test of this weapon with a somewhat negative attitude because of the weight and cost of this system. These ideas were quickly dispelled when we began the tests. Anyone who really understands killing or the problems involved in the use of deadly force to terminate the actions of a dangerous felon, will truly appreciate this weapon. To know that **extremely accurate** follow-up shots are right there at your fingertips, **without** taking your eyes off the target, at any distance, is very reassuring. Shoot this weapon, and you will understand. A **ten-round** string in **18 seconds** that produces a **1″ group** at 100 yards is very convincing.

M40A1 — Currently in use by the USMC and some Federal agencies. A highly customized Remington 700 action with heavy barrel, McMillan stock and 10X Unertl scope.

M40 A1 with 10x UNERTL scope

Heckler and Koch PSG-1 Sniper Rifle. A complete system with tri-pod, adjustable stock, five- and twenty-round magazines, the 6x42 Hensoldt bullet-drop compensating scope, illuminating reticle and a robust travel case. Undoubtedly the finest semi-automatic sniper rifle on the market today.

9

The Robar SR-90 is an excellent example of a state-of-the-art sniper rifle. The SR-90 has a specially designed, 3-way adjustable stock; match-grade Schneider fluted stainless steel barrel (1 in 12 twist); modified Remington trigger; and is available in .308Win. or .300 Winchester Magnum. This particular rifle is topped with a 10x Leupold MK4 (ultra).

McMillan M86SR with urban camo stock, McMillan action, Harris bi-pod and Leupold's Ultra 10x-M1 scope. The 86LR (long range) is similar but comes with a longer action in .300 WIN MAG. Stocks are also available in desert or woodland camo or plain black.

McMILLAN M-86. Gale McMillan's latest sniper rifle consists of the McMillan action, trigger and stock, the 1 in 12 stainless 24″ polygon barrel and an Ultra 10x-M1 scope. This system comes complete with case, bi-pod and cleaning gear. Gale is encouraging individuals to have the action glued into the stock for maximum consistency.

M82 — This is the commercially available sniper rifle built by Gale McMillan and the closest thing to an M40A1. The M82 is available with a Remington 700 or McMillan action, a 1 in 12 stainless, polygon barrel, fiberglass stock and Ultra 10X-M1 scope. Guaranted less than 0.5MOA accuracy.

McMillan sniper rifle built for the U.S. Navy.

M21 — Sniper version of the M14/M1A. An excellent rifle but not available outside the military. A custom built, **super-match M1A** from **Springfield Armory** is the next best thing. The author's rifle consistently groups under one inch at 100 yards using **Federal Match** ammo. The **Hart** heavy barrel and **Bishop** laminated stock definitely have a lot to do with this accuracy, not to mention that it was bedded and assembled to **MTU** standards.

Springfield M1A

ROBAR SR-60. Robbie Barrkman has fast established himself as a first class builder of sniper rifles. McMillan stocks, Schneider barrels, Remington actions, Leupold optics and Robbie's skill all go to make a rifle that is guaranteed to shoot half minute groups.

Robar SR-60

Take a look at the **FBI** statistics relating to sniper situations in the U.S. and you will see that there is a more economical approach to a sniper weapons system. There have been some 30-plus incidents in the last two years, mostly in the 70-90 yard range, and nearly all resulting in one-shot incapacitations.

There have been enough incidents of light bullets (.243, .223 and 25-06) fragmenting on glass or body tissue, with **less** than satisfactory results, to convince us that **.308 Win.** is the optimum choice.

VARMINT RIFLES

This is a very practical and cost effective way to get a quality weapon. These include the heavy barrel Remington 700BDL, Winchester 70 and the Ruger77V.

Although we have had a few of these that have shot very well out of the box we still recommend a few low-cost modifications:

- **FLOAT THE BARREL — at least** one sixteenth of an inch clearance. Two business cards should slide between barrel and fore-end easily. Any less will result in contact points during recoil vibration, or wood swell from humidity.
- **BED THE ACTION —** preferably by a gunsmith experienced in high-power rifle work or by using **ACRAGLAS** kit from Brownells.
- **CLEAN UP THE TRIGGER PULL** — most are adjustable (2-3 lbs.).
- **LOCTITE THE SCOPE MOUNT AND RING SCREWS.**
- **PARKERIZE OR TEFLON THE BARREL AND ACTION.**
- **DULL THE HIGH GLOSS STOCK FINISH.**

Winchester Mod 70 and H&K 93

HUNTING RIFLES

Many agencies have deer rifles in their armories that can either be traded in or upgraded.

A good action can be **re-barrelled** with a quality heavy barrel, re-stocked with a fiberglass stock and after **floating** and **bedding** will shoot as well as any factory sniper weapon.

TARGET RIFLES

There are two target rifles worth considering, the **Remington 40XB** and **the Steyr Match**. Both very accurate out of the box.

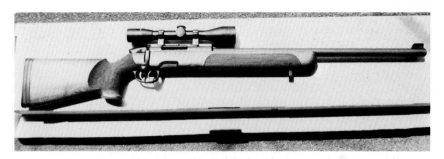

Steyr SSG-Match with ZF-69 scope.

CUSTOM RIFLES

Many fine rifles are built in this manner. Take a strong reliable action (REM.700, WIN.70 or SAKO), add a premium heavy barrel (**Douglas, Hart** or **Shilen**), a good trigger (**Timney** or **Canjar**), bed it all into a fiberglass stock (**McMillan, Brown Precision**), mount a good scope (**Leupold**), add butt pad and sling system and you will have one of the finest rifles available.

Contact someone like **Gale McMillan**, or any reputable gunsmith to have all or part of the work done. It is not a very large or difficult job but select a gunsmith with a sound background in building precision rifles. A good weapon can be built for between $800 and $1200, depending on the optional extras.

Custom McMillan/Sako scoped with the Zeiss 2.5x-10x.

13

BARRELS

The quality of the barrel is a critical part of accuracy. When a weapon is well used and begins to lose the accuracy it once had, rebarrelling is the best solution ($300 approx.). The **Hart, Douglas** or **Schneider** in 1-10, 1-11 or 1-12 twist, stainless is a good choice for .308Win. (22"-24")

Likewise, if a weapon never attains the standard you seek the barrel is probably the problem. Provided of course the bedding and floating were done correctly.

Lack of cleaning and metal fouling may also be a cause of loss of accuracy. See the section on **CLEANING** IN THIS BOOK.

Incorrect cleaning can be more detrimental than a lot of shooting. The biggest danger is damage to the last inch or two of the rifling in the muzzle, caused by running the cleaning rod **off center.**

On occasions we have improved accuracy immediately by simply having the barrel **professionally** shortened an inch or more.

Shortening the barrel can make the weapon more maneuverable in tight spaces and easier to climb with. We have one rifle with a Douglas 1 in 10 barrel, shortened to 19 inches which shoots consistent cold shots and groups less than **half an inch** at 100 yards.

It is a good idea to have the crown, at the muzzle end of your barrel, slightly **recessed** to protect it from damage.

After having a new barrel fitted, have the gunsmith show you that the **headspace** is correct by using **go/no-go gauges. Headspace** is the **most important** dimension governing the **safety** of the shooter.

M40A1 Recessed crown

SSG crown

STOCKS

If you decide to restock your weapon, either for accuracy or simply because the old one is cracked, go with a new **fiberglass** or **Kevlar** unit. For $150-$200 it is well worth the expense and will probably be cheaper than a new wood one. Camouflage, recoil pad, sling swivels and bedding will all cost a little extra.

There are a lot of low-grade fiberglass stocks on the market, so go with a good one like **McMillan, Robar** or **H-S.**

More important than the composition of the stock, wood or fiberglass, is the **way it is bedded.** It has been seen that even synthetic stocks, like the one on the SSG, can warp in direct sunlight and heat. **Laminated walnut** stocks have long been a favorite of many great shooters and are an excellent alternative to fiberglass.

A wood stock can also be stabilized by **epoxy impregnation** under pressure and heat, but this is not a common process.

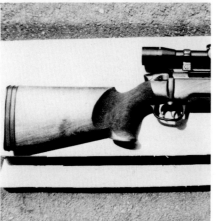

Above left: Robar Desert Camo

Above: Fully adjustable PSG-1 stock

Left: Pad extension/spacers on Steyr SSG Marksman

BEDDING

Before you rush out for a new stock, consider having the existing one properly bedded. This consists of removing some wood from the inside of the stock and replacing it with bedding compound to give a **tight** and **moulded** fit to the barrel and action. We like to bed **one inch** forward of the action, underneath the barrel. If it is a wood stock, you will want to hog out the fore end under the barrel and glass it too. Be sure to maintain your floating or clearance under the barrel. This procedure will prevent the wood swelling and coming up to touch the underside of the barrel.

Pillar bedding has considerable advantages over conventional bedding and should be used where possible. This consists of drilling out and enlarging the action mounting bolt holes and sleeving them with aluminum tubes and bedding compound. This will reduce crushing of the bedding when **torquing** the bolts.

The primary area to bed is the **recoil lug,** but the sides and back of the action should also be done. Have a competent gunsmith do this, preferably one that has done a lot of High Power or Bench Rest rifle work.

For a more complete guide to the bedding process read the instructions that come with **Brownell's Acraglass** bedding kit. If you are at all competent with small hand tools you may want to try bedding your own weapon. We would suggest you practice on one of your old hunting rifles before attempting a precision sniper weapon. Do not try to rush the process and give the compound ample time to cure before shooting.

Two other excellent bedding compounds used extensively in the industry are **Micro-Bed** and **Devcon**.

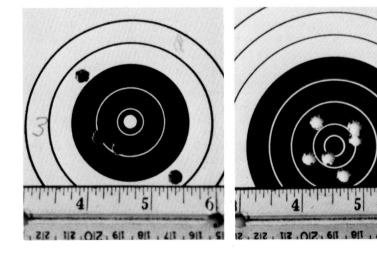

Shot with .243 Winchester Mod. 70, before and after bedding and floating (factory ammo).

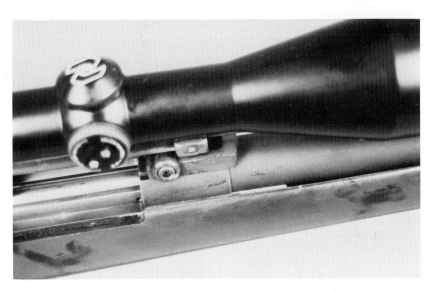

Note float gap and bedding between barrel and stock.

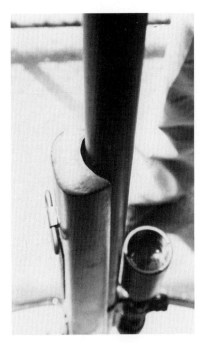

Floating on M40A1

At least two or three cards should slide between barrel and forestock.

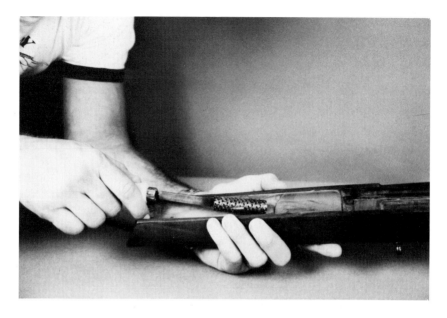

Useful rasp for removing wood from the barrel channel

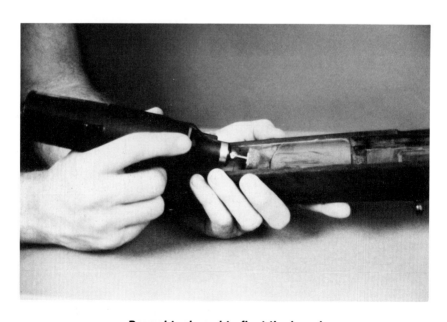

Dremel tool used to float the barrel.

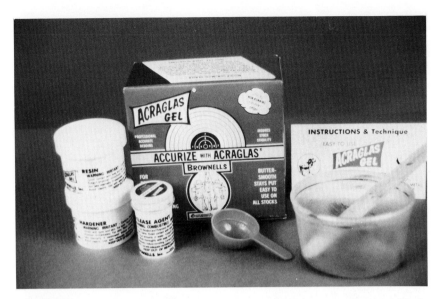

Acraglas kit from Brownells. It is still recommended that a good gunsmith do the bedding on an issue weapon. Other good bedding compounds are Micro-Bed and Devcon.

Bedding rear of action

Bedding around the recoil lug and the start of the barrel.

TRIGGERS

The suggested trigger weight for a sniper weapon is between **2-pound** and **4-pound**. It should not be so light that you may have accidental or premature discharges. At the same time, it should not be so heavy that you pull the shot off target when trying to break the shot quickly.

As you get better and become more familiar with your weapon you may start seeking a lighter trigger. There are two options: have a gunsmith rework the existing trigger mechanism or replace it with a new one(**Timney** is one possibility). A new trigger may cost $50-$150 so do not rush right into one until the existing one has been lightened or adjusted.

Avoid the double set triggers as found on some Steyr weapons. They are not only too light but some bench rest shooters have found that by loading or setting the springs they can actually disturb the weapon when released on firing.

Double triggers on SSG

The preferred single trigger on SSG P-II

SLINGS

At one time everyone believed the sling was only for carrying the weapon and that the bi-pod was the ultimate support. The bi-pod does have its place in sniper training but a good **sling position** is just as stable and more flexible in many ways.

Select a wide sling that will not cut off the circulation to the upper arm when in a full sling position. Leather is one of the best choices but be sure to avoid some nylon slings that may stretch under tension. Combined with a **glove** and **hand-stop** one can utilize the sling in all positions.

Rail installed in SSG P-II

Custom handstop and bi-pod rail mount made by Joe Wagner of Los Angeles.

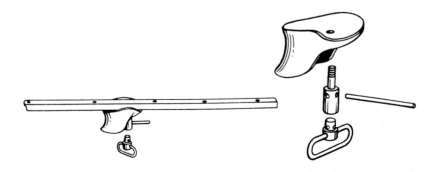

Two examples of Freeland's handstops and rail mount.

10x-M1 Click adjustments

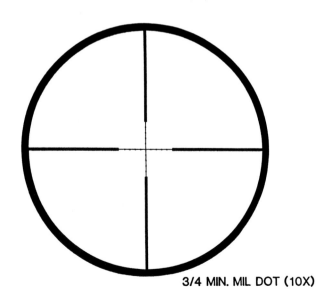

3/4 MIN. MIL DOT (10X)

5
SCOPES

The scope is a critical part of the sniper weapons system; it is also the most prone to damage.

The scope should be a strong, high quality unit with ample **field of view,** good **magnification** for target identification and light gathering. It should not be adversely affected by recoil, weather or **reasonably** rough handling.

FIXED OR VARIABLE POWER

Again a subject that has many pros and cons.

Fixed is simpler, stronger, less versatile but more than adequate. The **USMC** favors the 10X Unertl on their M40A1 and Leupold have the excellent 10X ULTRA but some units prefer the 6X Kahles for its field of view.

The **Leupold ULTRA** series of scopes are probably the best made in the USA specifically for sniper application. The **10X-M1** has the external click adjustment for exact targeting at specific ranges and is also available in 16X and 20X. The **10X-M2** ($450 approx.) has friction adjustments and low profile caps for more rugged application. The **M2** is available to law enforcement and military with a range finding reticle (stadia lines), which operate on the width of a man's shoulders at the specific range indicated.

All the ULTRAs are machined aluminum with a wall thickness of 0.100", **waterproofed** (actually locked out of a submarine in one test) and matte finished.

The 10X is better for **facial identification** of a target, keeping in mind that barricade suspects have changed clothes with the hostages in the past.

Variable power has some advantages. One can use low power at very close range and higher powers for target identification and shooting at longer range. We have encountered variable scopes that change shot placement with power changes. The **NRA** tests indicated that Leupold was one of the best units for not causing this error. Be sure to shoot your scope on **all powers** to try and find this problem.

One of the best features of a variable scope is its **light gathering** at low powers. You can wind it down and see when a more powerful setting would inhibit vision.

Good variables are **3-9, 2-10, 4-12** ranges, but this does not rule out other combinations. The **US Army** selected the **ART II, 3X-9X** for their M21, the French **GIGN** selected the **Zeiss 2.5X-10X** for their sniper systems.

We have found our best shooting in the 8X and 10X range but it is nice to have the lower powers for scanning and observing. One of the best economical scopes we have found, and are currently using on two of our weapons, is the matte finished **3X-9X Leupold** with the **duplex reticle** (under $200). Weaver and Redfield both have similar scopes available.

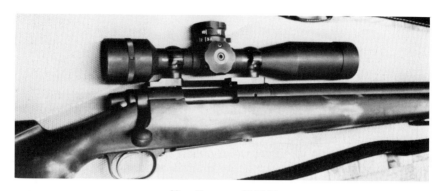

Unertl on an M40A1

Leupold Ultra 10x-M1 on a U.S. Navy/McMillan

Ultra 10x-M2

Hensoldt 6x42 PSG-1

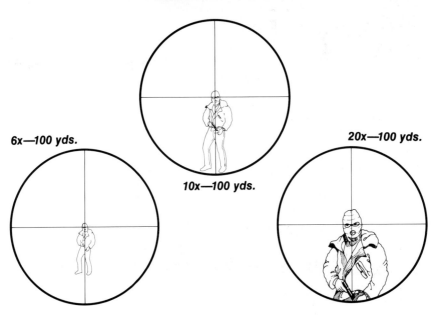

6x—100 yds.

10x—100 yds.

20x—100 yds.

Various power settings at 100 yds. Drawn to scale.

Kahles ZF69 on an SSG Marksman. Note the quick release mounts.

Second screw in M1A/M14 mount improved the accuracy of this system.

RETICLES

The **duplex** reticle has become the most popular and most practical for sniper work. It is easy to see in low light, fast to pick-up but capable of precise shot placement on the cross hairs. Avoid reticles with **too fine** cross hairs; they are almost impossible to see in low light conditions. The same is true for **very pointed** post sights; the point becomes obscure, resulting in major errors in shot placement. The **flat top** post is too broad and covers the target as do the cross wires with **dot.**

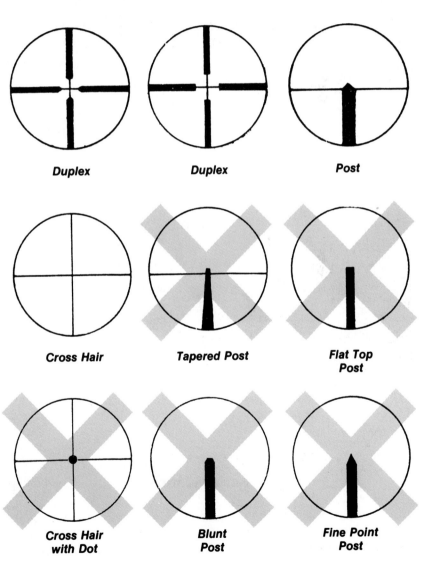

Duplex   Duplex   Post

Cross Hair   Tapered Post   Flat Top Post

Cross Hair with Dot   Blunt Post   Fine Point Post

RANGE FINDERS

Along with **bullet drop compensators,** range finders are a nice feature on a military scope but not necessary for short to medium range police work. They work on the principle of placing two lines over a known distance, **neck to belt** or **shoulder to shoulder** and then reading off the range. Most times in law enforcement application one only sees partial targets obscured by windows and hostages, so it is all but impossible to get an accurate reading. Learn to estimate range and know your weapon's dope.

If your agency does require this long-range option, the bullet drop compensator of the **ULTRA 10X-M1** or the range finder of the **10X-M2** would be worth testing. We have also found the system on the **H&K PSG-1** a pleasure to work with for long-range sniping.

Other range finders requiring parallel lines, adjustments and range boards in the scope only tend to clutter the sniper's view.

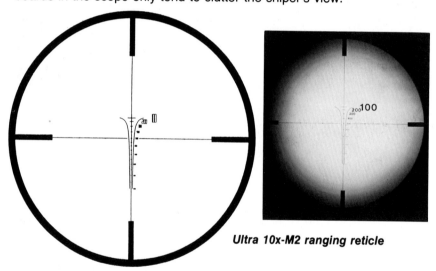

Ultra 10x-M2 ranging reticle

SCOPE MOUNTING

The mounts and rings should be strong, high quality units compatible with both scope and rifle. Be aware that some scopes utilize a 30mm tube (**Leupold Ultra, Kahles, Zeiss**) and some a 1″ tube. Make sure you can get the matching rings.

After mounting, all screws should be pulled up tight and secured with some **locking compound** to prevent them vibrating loose, then their positions recorded in the sniper log book.

The eye relief can be set at this time (distance from shooter's eye to scope), **3″**—3½″.

Snipers must maintain their equipment and learn to recognize movement in the sighting system. A **small** error or movement in the mounts will result in a **major** error in shot placement.

Eye relief is usually 3"-3½" between shooter's eye and the scope.

CLICK ADJUSTMENTS

Most teams zero their weapons for one distance **(100 yards)** then use hold-over or hold-under for other distances. But if you prefer to make click adjustments be sure the scope consistently returns to zero when making readjustments.

The clicks should be in ¼" **rather than** ½" graduations and be both positive and audible.

Take your scope, zero for 100 yards, now move the elevation up 20 clicks then down 20 clicks and see if you are still zeroed. Some scopes are designed for this and some are not. Generally the higher quality target scopes, with **micrometer** adjustment knobs, perform this task the best. The large knobs that come with this type of scope may get damaged in your climbing and crawling, so consider the range you will be working at before investing in one of these units.

Remember to **log** your clicks for various distances and log the last zero on the weapon at the end of practice. There should be no confusion if you are called out on an operation as to what distance your system is zeroed for. Most snipers log this information on a piece of tape on the side of the weapon, just to be sure.

ADJUSTABLE OBJECTIVE

You will also see this written as **AO**. This is an adjustment found on scopes to eliminate the errors of parallax, by focusing the objective image on the reticle. It is worth the few extra dollars to get this feature on a new scope.

The sniper may be called upon to shoot at **40 yards** or **150 yards.** Without **AO** he will not have a clear picture up close and may not be able or willing to take the shot.

A.O., adjustable objective shown on a Leupold scope.

Click adjustment on a Zeiss. 1 click = 1 cm at 100 meters.

NIGHT SCOPES

Night scopes are an expensive but excellent piece of equipment, since many teams are given the **Green Light** during the hours of darkness when the hostage takers are on their lowest alert.

Avoid the old military surplus **Starlight** type scopes and go with the newer generation of scopes like the units from **Litton (M-845).** They are more compact, less prone to damage and give a clearer sight picture. ($5,000 approx.)

It is best to have one rifle **permanently** set up with a night vision system to avoid switching scopes and possible losing your zero at a critical point in an operation.

Night scope and laser designator on H&K G3

Night scope with internal laser designator on an Israeli Galil.

View through a night scope at midnight.

COLLIMATOR

The collimator, or **Professional Boresighter** (as made by **Bushnell**), is another useful accessory that will more than pay for itself in saved ammunition. The unit is placed in the end of the barrel with an adjustable arbor and used to align the bore with the scope. It **does not zero** the weapon but it will get you on target immediately and save the unnecessary waste of ammo.

Once the weapon is zeroed, replace the collimator and record the position of the reticle on the grid inside the boresighter. Now, when called out on an operation you have an instant method of checking your weapon's zero without firing a shot. Very important if the weapon was roughly handled or dropped while deploying.

Collimator

Collimator in use on a custom McMillan/Sako.

32

6
SONIC SUPPRESSORS

A useful tool for some teams but not an essential item. A good silencer will not have an adverse effect on accuracy at close range and will allow a sniper to get off two or three shots before the opposition realizes they are under fire. In fact, a good suppressor can improve accuracy since it is lowering the exit pressure of the gases behind the projectile. It also reduces felt recoil and noise, thus becoming easier on the sniper.

Silencers work best with bolt action weapons and also double as excellent flash suppressors. Although not a consideration during the day, **muzzle flash** can be a dead give-away at night.

Again, like the night scope it is not an item that can be taken on and off a weapon system and still supply satisfactory performance. There are a few companies that specialize in suppressed sniper weapons and market an excellent product.

There are both high velocity and sub-sonic suppressors, so do not assume that you must use special ammunition to utilize the "can."

Use an alignment rod any time the suppressor is moved or replaced. **"Should be OK"** is not good enough at 2000-plus feet per second.

The weapon should also be **rezeroed** any time the suppressor is moved.

A suppressed .22 long rifle weapon is very useful for eliminating dangerous animals or shooting out lights when they interfere with an operation.

Suppressor and night scope on an Israeli M26.

33

Suppressor mounted on the "Bull-Pup" Sirkis M36 (Israel).

Harris bi-pod attached to PSG-1 using the custom handstop/rail mount made by Joe Wagner.

7
BUDGET

The following prices are only intended as a guide for those individuals required to make proposals or budgets for sniper equipment. The prices used are **approximations** and subject to **change** without notice from the suppliers.

RIFLES (scopes not included)

Remington 700BDL Varmint	$400+
Remington 40XB	$800+
Winchester 70, VarminT	$400+
Steyr SSG	$700+
Steyr SSG-P11	$800+
Steyr Marksman	$1000+
M86	$2400+ complete with scope
McMillan	$1200
M40A1	$2400 complete with scope
H&K PSG-1	$5900+ complete with scope
Robar	$2475
Springfield M1A, Supermatch	$1000+
Sako, Heavy Barrel	$750+

GUNSMITHING

Bedding & Floating	$40+
Rebarrel	$300+ with barrel
Restock	$200–$350 with stock
Trigger work	$30+ not including new trigger
Trigger	$50+
Recoil pad fitted	$40 with pad
Parkerize or Polymax	$100–$150
Bi-pod	$40+
Handstop and rail	$30+

SCOPES

Leupold 3-9	$160+
Leupold 3.5-10 AO	$180+
Leupold 10X-M2 ultra	$700
Zeiss Sniper	$800+
Kahles ZF 69, ZF 84	$1000+
Mounts & rings	$40–$120
Litton night scope	$5000+

AMMO

Federal Match 168gr BTHP .... $350 per case of 500

ACCESSORIES

Freeland shooting mat $66
Shooting glove .... $20-$30
Sling .... $20-$30
Shooting jacket .... $100+
Three-point stand .... $60+
Sand bags .... $5+
Bushnell Boresighter $55
Cleaning equipment .... $30+
Rifle case .... $70+

Steyr A.U.G. (Army Universal Gun). Scope is incorporated in the top "handle."

8
SECONDARY WEAPONS

Apart from their handgun, many snipers have begun carrying a second rifle. Generally a semi-automatic assault rifle with a scope option (**AR15, H&K 91, H&K 93**) especially if they do not have a sniper/observer to handle their security or additional firepower.

This weapon would be used where the **volume** of cover fire or suppressing fire is more important than **precision.**

This is not to say that the secondary weapon is not accurate, it should still hold **2-3 inch** groups at 100 yards with a scope sight.

The secondary weapon would become the sniper's primary weapon where the situation did not allow or require the normal deployment of a sniper (e.g. inside a high-rise, large warehouse or hospital).

This weapon should be issued with at least three extra 20-round magazines, sling, log book and cleaning gear. The scope for this weapon would be in the fixed 4X category with a wide field of view.

One major SWAT unit on the West Coast has a very good system, the sniper/observers are issued two weapons, the **H&K 33 (5.56mm)** for firepower and support, and a bolt action **Remington 700 (.308)** with X3-X9 scope for precision sniper work when needed. Primary snipers are issued the **H&K G3SG1 .308 (7.62mm)**.

H&K 93 (5.56 mm)

SPECIALTY WEAPONS

A .22 rimfire, set up with a scope, can be a useful training aid with many advantages such as cost, noise and recoil. It can also be used on an indoor range where a high-powered rifle generally cannot.

Equipped with a silencer and sub-sonic ammunition, it can be very useful on troublesome animals and wildlife without disturbing the neighborhood with gunfire.

Another special weapon is the handgun or sub-machine gun set-up with scope and bi-pod for close-in sniping. These could be used inside large buildings or aircraft. The French use a 6″ revolver in .38 special for this purpose, but in the U.S. the **H&K 94** is becoming very popular.

94 SG 1
9mm Para
15
16.54″
6 Groove Conventional
10″ RH
40.38″
7.18 lbs.
Matte black phosphated
Fixed
Luepold (6x) fixed

HK 94 SG-1 Marksman's Rifle

H&K 94 SG-1 marksman's rifle.

H&K 94 (9mm), the semi-automatic version of the MP5.

Clark .45 ACP with Aimpoint Scope

9
AMMUNITION

GENERAL ISSUE

As many sniper rifles as there are on the market, there are even more brands and types of ammunition. The basic rule is to obtain the ammunition that performs best in your rifle, not the cheapest that the agency could find.

Over the years, much testing and improvement has been done with the **.308 WIN (7.62 NATO)** round. The military has developed very accurate match ammunition for their competition and sniper teams (Lake City Match). We also have excellent products available on the civilian/police market, namely **Federal Match** loaded with the **168 grain Boat Tail Hollow Point.** One has to be very precise on the loading bench to beat the accuracy of this ammunition.

Look for **Winchester-Western's** new 168 grain match ammo soon. They will be loading the **Sierra BTHP** match projectile.

If you are not using .308 WIN then buy several different brands and see which performs best in your weapon. Heavier bullets seem more stable at long range but the twist of your barrel will also be a factor.

Try to purchase large quantities of the **same** lot number to ensure consistency in your ammo. If it becomes necessary to change lot numbers, brands or types of ammunition be sure to **re-zero** all sniper weapons. Higher quality ammunitions seem to have very consistent performance from lot to lot but if your agency has purchased for economy and not for quality you may notice more variation.

If you are a small agency, coordinate your purchases with other agencies in your area to obtain the larger quantity of match grade ammo for the best price.

A chronograph can be very useful for testing the quality and consistency of different ammo lots. Some agencies will put exceptional lots aside specifically for the use of their sniper teams.

Store your ammo in a **cool, dry, stable** environment and when on location, keep your spare rounds out of the sun. Hot rounds mean higher pressure and higher velocity, so higher impact.

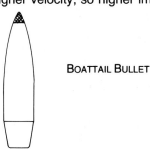

BOATTAIL BULLET

SPECIALTY AMMUNITION

Many agencies like to keep various special munitions on hand; Armored Piercing, Tracer, Ball, etc.

A.P. is useful for shooting engine blocks to disable vehicles.

If this is your agency's policy be sure to test and log your training results with these different projectiles.

You will need to know either the click adjustments on your scope or the hold-off to get the same results as your regular issue ammunition.

For long-range application in .308 consider the **Lapua 185 grain Match** or **Sierra 190 grain Match King.** Another popular alternative is the **300 Winchester Magnum** cartridge.

CUSTOM AMMO

Most serious marksmen and competition shooters will experiment with custom loaded rounds to get the ultimate performance out of their rifles, with excellent results. When **Delta Team** snipers began hand loading their own rounds, 3 hours a day, they became more careful in their shooting, and proficiency increased. This was back in '78 when good factory ammo was harder to come by and they were using the **40XBs** built by **Remington.**

Hand loading is very economical from a component cost standpoint but not from a time invested one.

From our experience, the time required to hand load premium rounds is not justified with the high standard and excellent accuracy we have found in the factory **Federal Match** ammunition.

If you do have the time and inclination to "roll your own" for your rifle, you will be pleased with the results. Here are a few helpful hints:

1) Follow the directions in a good reloading manual.
2) Use new or once fired cases.
3) Check and trim all cases to length.
4) Weigh powder charges carefully.
5) Use the **Sierra** or **Hornady Match** 168 grain BTHP.
6) Seat projectiles to the maximum overall length that will still fit and function in your weapon.

With careful loading and a little practice you will be shooting ¼″ - ½″ groups. True consistency only comes with hand loading but it is very time consuming. If you do want to have Armored Piercing rounds in your inventory you can hand-load the projectiles to perform similar to your issue ammunition.

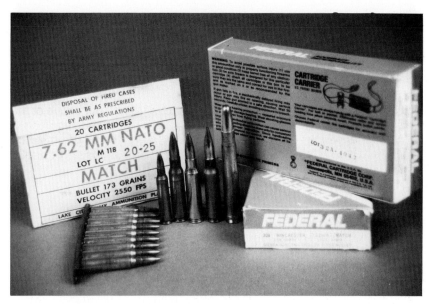

L. to R.: Stripper clip of 5.56mm, .223 Rem, 7.62 Nato, Federal Match .308 Win, .308 Win handload and 375 H&H Magnum.

MATCH LOAD

The author, and many military match shooters, utilize the following data:

40 grains of **DUPONT IMR 4895,** loaded behind the **SIERRA 168 grain BTHP** match bullet (or **HORNADY's 168 gr BTHP).**

Seat the bullets to the maximum length that will fit and function in the magazine of your weapon. The less distance the bullet must travel before it meets the rifling, at the chamber end of the barrel, the better. Use a light crimp so that the projectiles are not pushed back into the case by the recoil of previous rounds.

The **IMR 3031** powder is also an excellent choice; 39 grains behind the 168 grain bullet has proved very successful.

WARNING: FOLLOW THE DIRECTIONS, WARNINGS AND TABLES IN A GOOD RELOADING MANUAL IF YOU DECIDE TO HAND-LOAD YOUR OWN AMMO!!

POLICY

As a final note you may want to consider your agency's policy with regard to the liability of using hand-loaded ammo. Our feeling is that you should only use fresh factory ammo, from the same lot number you were practicing with, for operations.

Federal and Military Match ammo are both loaded with the 168 grain BTHP. Note lot numbers on the boxes.

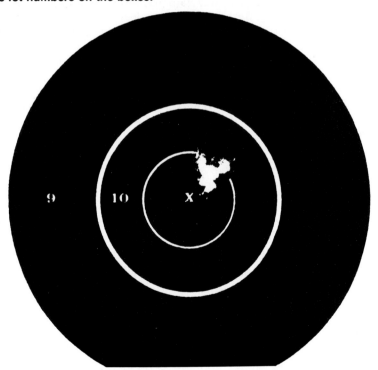

Actual group shot with Super Match M1A at 100 yards

10
TEST AND ZERO

The first job after purchasing or building a new sniper weapons system is to get it out to the range for test and evaluation. Begin with a 25-yard range in calm conditions. You will need to test the weapon without the hindrance of wind, rain, extreme heat or cold.

With the weapon you will require scope, sandbags, bi-pod, the best available ammo, cleaning rod, tool kit and log book.

If you can, purchase a good Bench Rest three-point stand and sandbag set. One for the whole team would be invaluable for testing weapon accuracy.

Another useful accessory is a bore-sighting **Collimator** like the one made by Bushnell. This allows an immediate alignment without firing a shot. Once the weapon is zeroed, it can serve as a quick way of checking your scope setting, prior to an operation.

Run a dry patch through the barrel to remove any possible oil or foreign matter, then begin by getting the weapon on the target at 25 yards. The paper work that came with your scope will tell you everything you need to know about the windage and elevation adjustments of your particular optical sight. A scope with a ¼″ click at 100 yards will only move $^1/_{16}$″ at 25 yards.

Now move to 100 yards and fine-tune your zero for **point of aim-point of impact.**

Now is the time to take your tools and check that all scope and stock mounting screws are still tight. A loose weapon will never arrive at true zero.

If all screws are tight, the action is well bedded and the barrel floated, you should now be able to shoot a sub-one inch group at 100 yards from a supported position. It is not difficult for a competent marksman with a good weapon to achieve this level.

Bench rest and sandbag for test purposes.

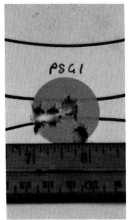

Three consecutive 5-shot groups shot from a PSG-1, prone tri-pod.

TROUBLE SHOOTING

If you never achieve this one-inch group it is time to evaluate your weapons system. Some of the common problems are:

• Low quality ammo
• Loose scope mounts
• Defective scope, broken reticle
• Loose stock mounting bolts
• Contact points under barrel (floating)
• Fouled or dirty barrel
• Worn or defective barrel
• Poor marksmanship

It is not difficult to trouble shoot a rifle, so if you are not sure, go to your sniper instructors or armorers for some help.

Assuming you achieve your zero at 100 yards and are grouping consistently around one inch, it is time to move on.

It is now time to begin logging the data on your weapon. See the sample page of a sniper's log book. Remember your **log book** may become a **legal document** required in a shooting investigation.

Group the weapon at 25, 50, 75, 100, 150, 200 and 300 yards. Accurately record the difference between your point of aim and the bullets' point of impact. You now have a good idea of the necessary **"hold-over"** or **'hold-under"** for the various distances you may be required to shoot at.

44

If time permits, go to the range each morning, put a patch through the barrel and fire your cold shot at 100 yards. If the weapon system is good your point of impact will be right on. Log the results and shoot four 5-shot groups. Again there should be no deviation.

Repeat this procedure as often as possible until you are 100 percent satisfied that you have a sound sniping system.

Once you have complete confidence in the weapons system you can begin your training in various positions, under various conditions and at various ranges. **Log all results.** Also, log any changes or adjustments made to the sights, rifle or ammunition. Mark and record screw head positions on the weapon.

The weapons system should be checked and re-zeroed after any alterations or when there is a change in ammo lots.

A good practice is to shoot 5 or 10 rounds out of a box of ammo at the end of training, then keep the other 10 or 15 with the weapon as your first selection on an operation. This is just one more piece of insurance that your weapon is zeroed for that particular lot number.

GROUPING

All groups for test purposes are measured from **center to center** of the **two most distant holes.** Or one can measure the outside edges of the two most distant holes and subtract the caliber of the bullet. Generally, test groups are shot over a solid bench rest with the weapon carefully sandbagged. For the purposes of this book, all groups shown or described, were shot either from a prone bi-pod position or prone sandbag.

We have found that the sandbag gives more accurate results, but since so many teams use the **Harris bi-pod** we would supply that data. The bi-pod tends to make weapons shoot a little higher if they were zeroed on a sandbag. So, whether you use bi-pod, sandbag or sling, zero your weapon in the position it will be deployed in the field.

10 rounds rapid fire, PSG-1.

McMillan/Sako

45

TORQUE WRENCHES

To really fine-tune your weapon you should use a torque wrench to set the stock/action mounting bolts. This way you can always ensure uniform tension in the system.

Always start torquing with the **front bolt,** in front of the magazine, and finish with the one behind the trigger guard.

Wood stocks can be torqued to 30-35 lbs.

Wood and glass bedded can go to 40-45 lbs.

Fiberglass and bedded to 55-60 lbs.

The M40A1 should be torqued as follows:

> 15 front, then 15 rear
> 30 front, then 30 rear
> 45 front, then 45 rear
> 55 front, then 55 rear

Some units that are pillar bedded can go to 65 lbs.

Some weapons have a third screw or bolt just forward of the trigger guard; this can just be snugged up tight.

All bolt tensions would be routinely checked during cleaning.

Allen bolts for M40A1. Always torque the front bolt first.

Note the paint mark on the screw slot to indicate screw movement from vibration or recoil.

46

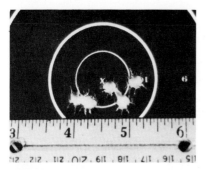

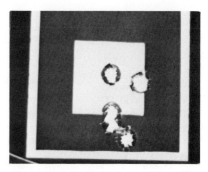

Five rounds prone unsupported with the M1A

Five round rapid fire from Steyr SSG.

Bench rest 3-point stand.

Note range data on the stock of this Parker Hale sniper rifle.

Bore guide and one-piece steel cleaning rod.

This is the best type of bore guide (made by Joe Wagner of Los Angeles). It is a close fit to the action and chamber and keeps the cleaning rod centered.

A custom tool used to clean the bolt locking lug recesses behind the chamber area.

Some useful tools for a sniper's kit.

11
CLEANING

There is a common misconception among shooters that it is no longer necessary to clean the bore of a weapon due to the non-corrosive priming of modern ammunition. The build-up of metal fouling from bullets passing through the barrel can greatly impair accuracy. Bench rest shooters who seek nothing but accuracy, clean their barrels after every tenth record shot.

The bolt should be removed and the bore cleaned from the breech end, with care taken not to cause damage or wear to the rifling at the muzzle end of the barrel. Instructions supplied with the cleaning agent should be followed carefully.

Use a one-piece steel cleaning rod **(Rig, Pachmayr),** or a plastic coated one like **Parker Hale's.** A folding rod should be kept in your pack for operations. A rod guide that fits into the breech can also save a lot of barrel wear from off-center cleaning.

There are two substances to clean from the bore: powder residue and copper fouling. The powder residue will come out easily with some form of carburetor cleaner or solvent, but the copper will require more attention.

Shooter's Choice is the best one step bore cleaner that we have found for maintaining our sniper rifles at peak accuracy. It will remove both powder and copper residue, and has none of the harmful side effects of ammonia solutions. The FBI recommends running the brush or jag tip up and back once for every shot fired since the last cleaning. Continue running patches through until no more green shows on the patch. If it is really bad you may have to swab the bore, then let it stand, muzzle down, for the night. Continue process in the morning.

Two conditions cause barrel wear: heat and dirt (friction).

It is suggested you swab the barrel after every **10 shots** in training; this will give the barrel a chance to cool and reduce copper build-up.

In actual fact, few snipers will clean their weapons during training, leaving this task until the end. A training session or Green Light competition will normally require 20 to 40 rounds shot over a four hour period, with ample time for barrel cooling between stages. We have sniper rifles that shoot hundreds of rounds between cleanings with no visible loss in accuracy. But this is not to suggest that more regular cleaning would not prolong the life of the barrel.

A barrel can last 15,000 rounds if properly cleaned and as little as 1,500 if not cared for. Your log will tell you if your groups begin to open up after 10,000 rounds or so. A Bench Rest shooter may get only 1,500 rounds through a barrel before he decides it is not competitive (¼″ groups). You may notice a change after 5,000 but not enough to junk the barrel.

A new or used rifle, acquired from unknown origins, should be thoroughly cleaned before testing accuracy. There is no way of knowing how many rounds were fired or how little it was cleaned before it got into your hands.

Use solvents and cleaning agents very sparingly; some of them will eat the Loctite or locking compound you should have used on your scope mounts. If your weapon is **Parkerized** or **Z-coated,** very little lubricant, if any, should touch the exterior of the weapon. Excessive oil in the action may be thrown back into your eyes during firing and thus make follow-up shots impossible.

Use only very clean, soft cloth for cleaning the scope lenses, or better yet, lens cleaners from your local camera shop.

Most snipers will leave a very light film of oil in the barrel when storing their weapons. Remember to clean this out with a dry patch before shooting or your first shot will be off the mark.

Keep oils and solvents off the bolt face as these may penetrate around the primer and cause a misfire.

A good rifle vise is an excellent accessory for bore cleaning. It will hold the weapon securely and allow you to really scrub that bore in a smooth, controlled manner.

Do not put your weapon away hot; it may sweat in the case. The new rubber scope covers have also been causing sweating. When a weapon is stored in a case, **inspect it periodically** for condensation and moisture.

The leather sling can also retain moisture and acids, so do not allow it to remain in contact with the metal parts of the weapon for prolonged periods.

It is a good idea to leave a card under the barrel, in the fore end channel, when casing the weapon. This way, when you take the weapon out next, you will simply run the card the length of the channel to ensure no **contact points** have formed under the barrel, and remove any dust or debris that may have gathered.

Always clean from the action end of barrel and be sure to use a bore guide.

12
ADDITIONAL EQUIPMENT

PERSONAL SWAT LOAD

Subdued Fatigue Uniform
Ball Cap/Wool Hat
Soft, Quiet Boots
Handgun & Extra Mags
Secure Holster
Gloves
Flashlight (small)
Gas Mask & Case
Ballistic Vest
Knife
Radio & Ear Plug
Smoke Grenade
Paper & Pencil
Camo Stick

SUPPORT PACK

Frameless Pack
Extra Ammo
Water
Food
Smoke Grenades
Poncho Cover
Sand Bags
Rope
Rappel Harness
Figure "8"
Carabiners
Tape

SNIPER LOAD

Rifle & Ammunition
Rifle Case
Sniper Log Book
Cleaning Rod
Dry Patches
Essential Tools
Shooting Jacket
Shooting Mat
Binoculars
Sniper Veil
Compass
Insect/Sun Screen
Streamlite Flashlight
Operational Log Book
Collimator

SNIPER TEAM SUPPORT GEAR

Spotlight System
Climbing/Rappelling Gear
Specialty Weapons & Ammo
Sand Bags
Full Tool Kit
Cold Weather/Rain Gear
Ladders
Three Point Stand
Night Scopes
Flares
Extra Batteries
Spare Radios
Tape Recorders

Individual SWAT load

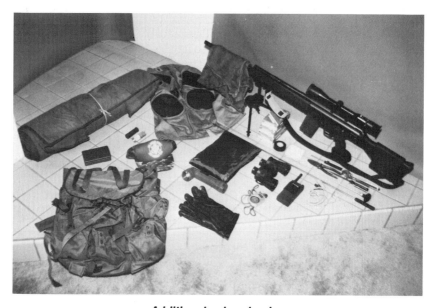

Additional sniper load

52

13
TRAVEL

Regardless of whether you are just transporting your weapons system to the range, travelling interstate like many federal agencies or travelling abroad like the military or Secret Service, you must have a strong and secure gun case.

The sniper weapon must be built rugged but handled with care. Do not throw it around just because it is in a good case.

THE CASE

The welded, heavy-duty aluminum cases are probably the best investment on the market but there are some excellent cases made from high density plastics as well.

Select a case that can be locked securely to ensure no one has decided to "check out the neat rifle" without your permission.

The case should have ample padding for the rifle with extra protection for the scope. There should also be room for the cleaning rod, some patches, the log book, possibly some ammo and adjustment tools.

We say "possibly some ammo" because some agencies do not like to store or transport weapons and ammo together.

Be sure that any extra gear in the case does not come in contact with the weapon.

AIR TRAVEL

Baggage handlers are notoriously rough on luggage, even when it is labeled "FRAGILE." If you can, personally hand load your Go Boxes, Equipment Bags and Weapons Cases on and off of the flight. If this is not possible, because of connecting flights, you may want to wrap the case with additional foam padding.

Separate the bolt and ammo from the weapon for security reasons. Also tape the joints around the case with heavy duct tape, to waterproof and discourage tampering.

ARRIVAL

If you are travelling for operational or competition reasons, try to fly a day early to give yourself time to re-zero the weapon upon arrival. There will be changes in temperature, altitude and humidity to account for, not to mention the fact that your weapon may have had a rough ride.

If you cannot arrive early, then you will have to depend on your collimator, log book and experience.

AMMUNITION

Take enough ammunition of the lot number you have been using, to last the entire visit without having to change to a new lot. If the situation requires a change in ammo find the time to re-zero your weapon.

McMillan case

Eagle drag bag + Robar SR-90

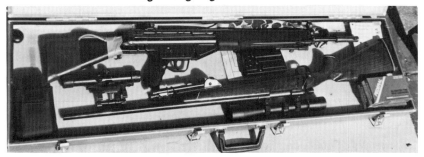

Cased Mod 70 and H&K 91

PART II

EDUCATION
AND
TRAINING

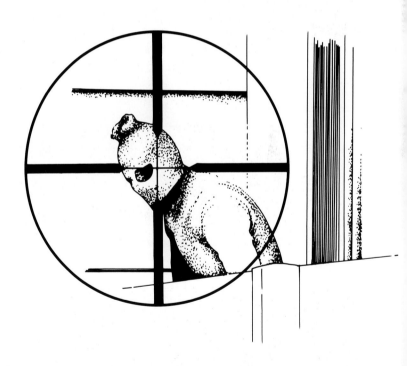

Rail and handstop on McMillan rifle.

Accuracy International Model "Moderated"

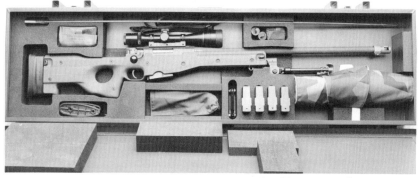

Cased Accuracy International "AW" with accessories

14
SNIPER EDUCATION

It is not the purpose of this book to teach **basic rifle marksmanship.** We are assuming that a sniper or sniper candidate is selected for his already excellent rifle skills.

Snipers are not taught to shoot; we simply show them how to apply their knowledge and skill to the role of sniper/counter sniper.

In reading this book there is no doubt that a novice shooter would learn many useful things about marksmanship, but this is information and training best received at the hands of a good rifle coach.

Probably the best learning experience we could recommend an officer, with an interest in being selected as a sniper, is to become involved in some form of **high power rifle competition.** The **NRA** can supply you with any information you may require on local competition, training programs or schools.

The other alternative is to set yourself up with your own personal sniper system and get out to the range and practice. The snipers in your agency will probably make you welcome when they see you are serious about this craft.

The next step is to convince your agency to send you to the one-week sniper school run by the FBI. After that it is more training and as many **Green Light Sniper Matches** as you can squeeze into your schedule.

Read as much as you can on rifle marksmanship, precision rifles, ballistics, field craft and SWAT/small unit tactics. Military personnel should research MOUT procedures (Military Operations in Urban Terrain). Obtain copies of the military sniper training manuals and study them carefully. Try to apply their methods to your operational requirements.

As we have said before, there is no substitute for hands-on experience, so get out to the range and practice.

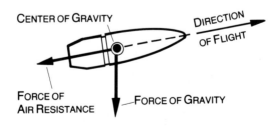

Forces acting on the bullet in flight

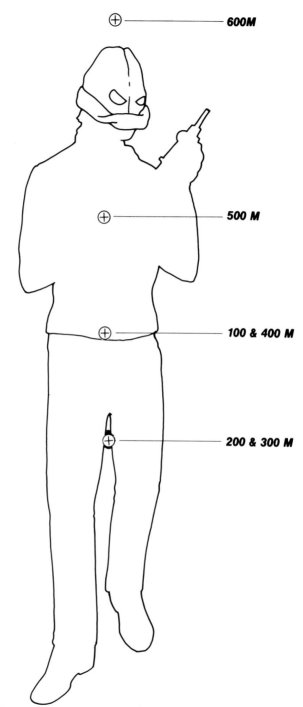

⊕ ———————————— **600M**

⊕ ——————— **500 M**

⊕ ——————— **100 & 400 M**

⊕ ——————— **200 & 300 M**

Military method —*correct aiming points for various ranges with sights set for 500 meters (7.62mm, national match ammo)*

15
BALLISTICS

Ballistics is the science which studies a projectile (bullet) in motion. It is divided into **Interior Ballistics**—from the start of primer ignition, through the rapid expansion of gases, the projectile's movement through the barrel until its exit from the muzzle; **Exterior Ballistics**—the bullet's flight from the muzzle to the target; **Terminal Ballistics**—the effect of the bullet's impact on the target.

INTERIOR BALLISTICS

An in-depth study of **Interior Ballistics** is not called for in a book of this nature but there are some points a sniper should be aware of. The first is Angle of Departure. Upon firing, the bullet begins to move down the barrel of the weapon setting up a vibration, and the vibration at the muzzle will influence the bullet's final line of departure. If this vibration is a constant and not affected by external forces, then the bullet will depart uniformly on each shot. These external forces could be different sling or grip pressures, contact with a barricade, foreign matter in the fore end channel or stock warpage and contact points.

The main thing to understand is that a heavy barrel vibrates less than a light one and by totally bedding the action and floating the barrel we reduce external forces to a minimum. Uniform grip and sling pressure and a soft rest are also important.

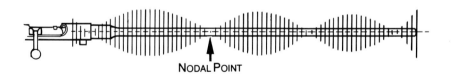

NODAL POINT

Barrel vibration during firing

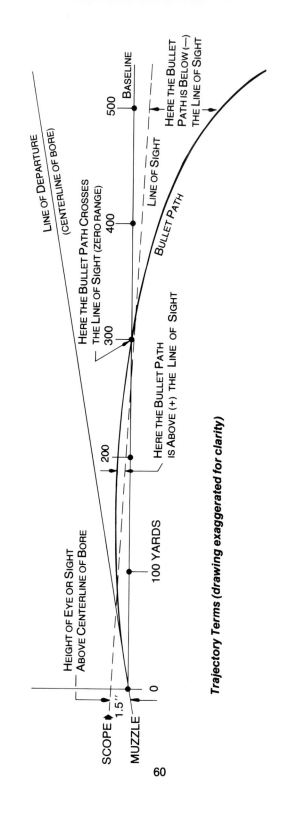

Trajectory Terms (drawing exaggerated for clarity)

LINE OF DEPARTURE
(CENTERLINE OF BORE)

BASELINE

HERE THE BULLET PATH IS BELOW (—) THE LINE OF SIGHT

HERE THE BULLET PATH CROSSES THE LINE OF SIGHT (ZERO RANGE)

LINE OF SIGHT

BULLET PATH

HERE THE BULLET PATH IS ABOVE (+) THE LINE OF SIGHT

500

400

300

200

100 YARDS

0

HEIGHT OF EYE OR SIGHT ABOVE CENTERLINE OF BORE

SCOPE

1.5"

MUZZLE

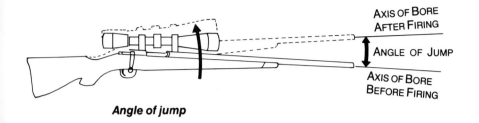

AXIS OF BORE
AFTER FIRING

ANGLE OF JUMP

AXIS OF BORE
BEFORE FIRING

Angle of jump

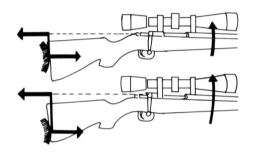

Dependence of the angle of jump on the shooter's position

EXTERIOR BALLISTICS

A knowledge of **Exterior Ballistics** is a little more important to the sniper. Here we deal with bullet weight and shape, air resistance, gravity and the bullet's flight line to the target (trajectory).

Effect of Sectional Density

Sectional density is the ratio of bullet weight to maximum cross-sectional area of the bullet.

Higher velocity will result in flatter trajectory if the bullets are identical but generally the higher velocity bullets are lighter. A bullet with a higher initial velocity and less sectional density will start with a flat trajectory but begin to drop fast after 300 yards (.222 for example). The bullet with lower initial velocity and greater sectional density will drop less over a longer range (.308Win). See diagram.

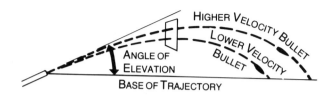

Effect of muzzle velocity on bullet range.

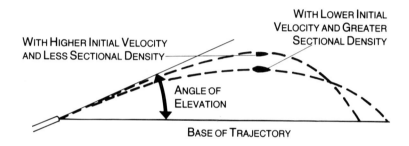

Effect of sectional density on range

Effect of Meterological Conditions

Lighter bullets will be more affected by wind and weather conditions than their heavier counterparts. This is another reason we recommend the .308Win over the lighter .222 and .223.

Medium Deflection

When a bullet passes through a medium such as glass, wood or steel we are concerned with three things: will it penetrate the medium, will it fragment and lose integrity, and how much will it be deflected. In all three cases the heavier bullets will perform more predictably and consistently. There are many horror stories from Vietnam of the **.223Rem, M16** bullets deflecting off of small twigs and branches in the jungle and having less than satisfactory effect on the enemy.

Some time back, the **FBI** took a shot through a bank window with a light .243Win and were very disappointed with the results. In all the tests we have done in shooting through mediums we can only conclude that anything less than .308Win is a gamble that your agency does not need.

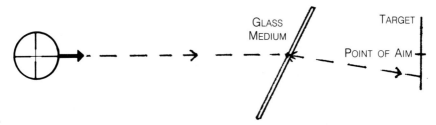

DEFLECTION EXAGGERATED FOR ILLUSTRATION

Although there are many variables involved: muzzle velocity, bullet design, type or thickness of glass, target distance from the glass, angle of bullet's impact with the glass, generally the bullet will deflect towards the perpendicular plane to the medium. Try to select a position as close as possible to 90 degrees to the medium, to minimize deflection.

TERMINAL BALLISTICS

For some insight into **terminal ballistics** one can compare the bullet effects on blocks of ballistic putty, gelatin or plastic water jugs. Anyone with considerable hunting experience will have had the opportunity to see the effect of various calibers on various animals.

There are no hundred-percent guarantees when shooting a suspect, but we can say that a shot to the head, center of mass, with a high velocity bullet will generally have an instant incapacitating effect. See the section on **Shot Placement** in this book.

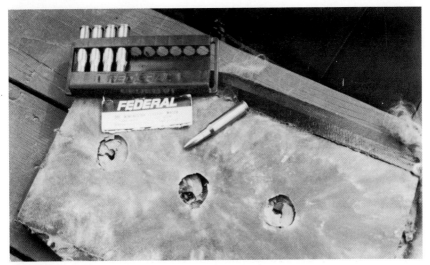

Total penetration of the High Threat Rifle Insert for a ballistic vest (.308 Win BTHP).

BALLISTIC DATA

It is very easy for the military sniper manuals to include a tremendous amount of ballistic data for their sniper trainees. The prime reason is that they all use the same rifle, the same scope and the same ammo.

This is not the case with law enforcement or specialized military teams. There is no standardization to base our data on. Everyone has different weapons with different barrel lengths, different calibers, ammunition manufacturers and ammo lots, different scopes and a wide variety of applications.

This is where the sniper must take his weapon system and log book, go to the range and develop his own data. Then if his unit uses the same equipment, he can print up the data and pass it along to the newer team members.

The prime data to develop is bullet drops at various ranges, moving target leads at various distances, bullet deflections from wind and bullet deflection through various types of glass from several angles. Also, possibly, penetration depths on various wood and steel barricades that may be encountered in the course of an operation.

The **FBI** Training Division can be a tremendous source of technical information and statistics in the area of sniper/counter sniper operations. But there is no substitute for experience, so get out there and approach your training with a scientific mind.

Some facts to be aware of:

Wind—can cause bullet deflection. You will need to know direction and speed to effectively calculate the hold-off.

Heat—Increased temperature means increased pressure. This will cause increased velocity and result in higher impact. Lower temperatures will work in the opposite direction.

Elevation—Higher altitude means thinner air, so less air resistance, resulting in higher bullet impact.

Humidity—Increased humidity means increased air density, so lower velocity and lower impact.

THE LOG

The above data dictates why it is essential to shoot under all possible conditions and log the results for future reference.

When the sniper finds himself deployed in a particular area, under unusual climatic conditions, he can refer to his **sniper's log book** to find a time where he trained under similar conditions and make the necessary adjustments in his point of aim before shooting.

Take advantage of hot or cold spells to get to the range and develop some new data on your weapons system. Shooting results from day and night, dusk and dawn should also be recorded.

SNIPER LOG

Date _____   Location _____
Temperature _____   Lighting _____
Time _____   Wind _____

Weapon _____   Ammo _____
Scope _____   Lot Number _____
Power _____

COLD SHOT

Position _____
Distance from POA _____
Adjustments _____

GROUPS

Distance from POA: _____

Range .... _____ _____ _____
Group Size _____ _____ _____

NOTES

Total shots fired _____

SPECIALIZED TACTICAL TRAINING UNIT

SAMPLE DATA

The following data is included as an example of what can be generated from 2½ hours of serious range work. It is not intended that the data be used for your weapons system, but only as a guide to developing your own data.

All shooting was done from a prone, bi-pod or tri-pod position under realistic field conditions.

The ammunition used was Federal 168 grain Match in .308Win and Federal 100 grain in .243Win. All groups are **5 shots** using the same point of aim and measured to the nearest 0.10".

The rifles used were:

H&K PSG-1: .308Win, 25.6" barrel, 6X bullet drop compensating scope and factory tri-pod.
Sako: .308Win, Sako action, 19" Douglas heavy barrel, Zeiss 2.5X-10X scope, McMillan stock and Harris bi-pod. Shooting on 10X.
Winchester: .243Win, Mod 70 Varminter, floated, bedded and set up with a Harris bi-pod. This was the final test of a new rifle that has never shot less than 1½" groups at 100 yards. It is currently being rebarrelled to .308Win.

Date: 29 April 86. Time: 0830-1100
Conditions: Warm, sunny, light tail wind.

100 YARDS:

PSG-1	Cold Shot	0.2" high
Sako	Cold shot	0.2" left
Mod 70	Cold shot	1.5" right (not acceptable)
Mod 70	Group	2.0" (not acceptable)

200 YARDS:

Weapons still zeroed for 100 yards.

PSG-1	POI 2.0" below POA	Group 1.2"
Sako	POI 4.5" below POA	Group 1.5"
Mod 70	POI 3.0" POA	Group 2.8"

PSG-1 scope set for 200 meters: POI=POA, Group 1.3"
Sako using calculated hold-over, placed 2 center head shots.

300 YARDS:

Weapons zeroed for 100 yards.

PSG-1	POI 12" below POA	Group 2.0"
Sako	POI 15" below POA	Group 2.5"

PSG-1 scope set for 300 meters: POI 2" above POA, Group 2.3"

AUTHOR'S NOTE:

The increased drop of the Sako can be explained by the shorter barrel and thus lower muzzle velocity. The important point is to know the exact hold-over or under for each individual weapon, at various distances. This can only be achieved by actual testing and recording of all shooting data.

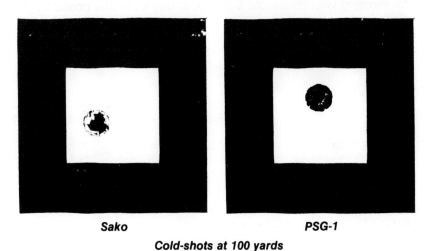

Sako   *PSG-1*

Cold-shots at 100 yards

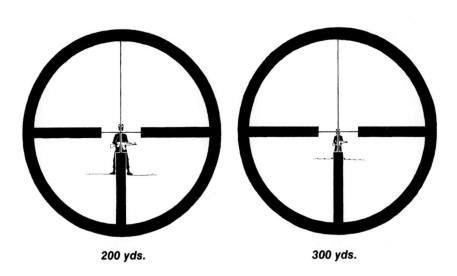

200 yds.   *300 yds.*

At 200 yds a low neck hold produced a good chest shot. At 300 yds. a high head hold gave the same result. Weapon zeroed for 100 yds.

Test through plate glass.

Test through car windshield.

16
ACCURACY

ACCURACY IS THE PRODUCT OF UNIFORMITY.

When all variables are constant, the weapon, the ammo, the shooter and the environment, the point of impact will always be the same. Now we know that it is impossible to achieve total uniformity, so we must endeavor to get as close as possible.

The following are some of the variables:

WEAPON
basic design
tightness of action
barrel quality and bore cleanliness
barrel temperature
floating and bedding
scope quality
scope mounting
all screw tensions
trigger release

AMMUNITION
brand and lot number
bullet design and weight
powder and charge
bullet seating depth
age and condition

ENVIRONMENT
wind direction and force
temperature and humidity
altitude and visibility
angle of shot

SHOOTER
physical and mental condition
body position and location
vision and breathing
sling tension, supported or unsupported
trigger release

When the sniper strives for perfection and uniformity, or at least **understands** the variables, he will achieve a high degree of accuracy in his shooting.

COMPOUNDING ERROR

Slight changes in **ONE** of the variables may result in a very minor deviation in shot placement but often several are at play.

For example, the shooter is very tired, he has eye strain and a headache; it is a very hot day, humidity is climbing and there is a brisk cross-wind, the light is fading; the weapon and ammunition have both been in the hot sun all day, he had to change ammo lot numbers and has not re-zeroed, the scope was knocked as he was climbing into position; the shooting position is not ideal, it is an up-angle shot with the sun behind the target; the shot will be through thin glass at a suspect holding a hostage close to his face.

Any **ONE** of these conditions could cause a slight change in bullet impact but all **COMPOUNDED** together could be a major error in shot placement. Quality equipment, intensive training and regular practice will give peace of mind.

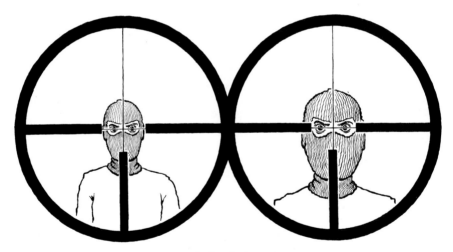

6x and 10x at close range

17
SHOOTING PRINCIPLES

POSITION

Create a stable base for your weapon. If you have the option of a rest or support, use it. Do not let the weapon system come in **direct contact** with **hard surfaces.** Get into the habit of shooting with a leather glove to protect your hand from rough concrete and splintered wood.

Your position should feel both comfortable and natural wherever possible. When you relax, the sights should not stray from the target, and when you breathe, the scope reticle should move vertically up and down through the point of aim. You may be there for a long time, so prepare your position well.

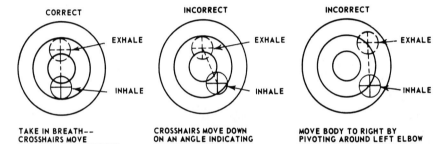

CORRECT

EXHALE

INHALE

TAKE IN BREATH--
CROSSHAIRS MOVE
STRAIGHT DOWN THROUGH
CENTER OF TARGET

INCORRECT

EXHALE

INHALE

CROSSHAIRS MOVE DOWN
ON AN ANGLE INDICATING
ELBOW NOT UNDER PIECE

INCORRECT

EXHALE

INHALE

MOVE BODY TO RIGHT BY
PIVOTING AROUND LEFT ELBOW
UNTIL CROSSHAIRS MOVE AS IN
EXTREME LEFT DRAWING

SIGHT PICTURE

This is relatively easy with a scope. The only skill required is to know your hold-over or hold-under for various distances. Remember, if you try to look through the scope and hold a sight picture for too long a period, your vision will blur and your eyes will become tired.

Even though the errors of parallax have been corrected in most modern scopes, still try to look through the center of your scope without the dark shadows becoming apparent on one side or the other.

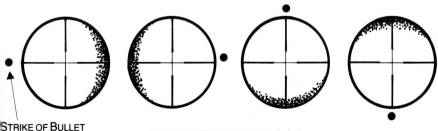

STRIKE OF BULLET

Shadow effects (scope sight)

BREATHING

This is a very important factor in precision rifle shooting. Keep in mind that the more powerful the scope the more this will magnify your movements. Even your heartbeat can cause a movement of the reticle on the target.

The technique is to breathe normally. When the shot is called for, exhale half your air, relax and squeeze off the shot. Ideally, the shot should break in **3-5 seconds;** if you go much past **8-10 seconds** you will begin to shake from lack of oxygen.

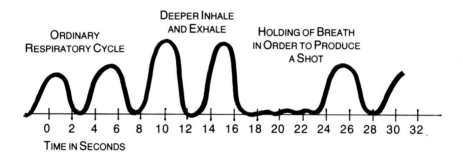

ORDINARY RESPIRATORY CYCLE

DEEPER INHALE AND EXHALE

HOLDING OF BREATH IN ORDER TO PRODUCE A SHOT

0 2 4 6 8 10 12 14 16 18 20 22 24 26 28 30 32

TIME IN SECONDS

Respiratory pause

TRIGGER CONTROL

This is the skill of releasing the trigger without the sights moving from the point of aim. A clean break can only be achieved by steadily building pressure on the trigger until you get a **"surprise"** break. Use the center of the first pad of your index finger.

Here is where we find the importance of a light, clean trigger. When the target may be visible for only a few seconds, it is important that the sniper get off a fast, clean shot with a minimum of disturbance to the weapon. Much practice may be called for, on the part of the marksman, to master the timing and safe release of a light trigger. The sniper should know his trigger well enough to be able to build pressure, hold, then break the shot instantly on command from the controller.

FOLLOW THROUGH

Immediately come back on target, chamber a fresh round and prepare for a second shot. Operate the bolt smoothly but sharply to eject the spent case cleanly.

18
SHOOTING POSITIONS

As stated earlier, always seek the position that will afford the best support for your weapon system and still supply cover and concealment for yourself.

A good **shooting jacket** with non-slip shoulder and elbow pads will improve shooting and comfort considerably. The jacket should fit snugly, have external equipment pockets and be of a subdued color. Even in warmer climates the sniper will find many advantages to using a padded shooting jacket.

The sniper should also have a padded **shooting mat** with some form of rubber or non-slip material under the elbow positions (Freeland's). This is extremely helpful when deployed on rough concrete or hot roofing materials.

A well designed **sling** is also an essential. A single point sling gives the best shooting results but two point slings will also improve the stability of the weapon in most shooting positions. The sling can be utilized in both supported and unsupported positions.

SUPPORTED

The most important factor in accurate supported shooting is **not to allow the weapon to come in direct contact with a hard surface.** The vibration and recoil, during firing, will cause the weapon to jump away from the hard surface and the shot to go astray.

A glove on the supporting hand will allow you to rest your hand between the weapon and a wall or support without the discomfort of a rough surface.

Many snipers are using the **Harris bi-pod** on their weapons with good results, but we still maintain that the **sand bag** is a superior method of support. The bi-pod is excellent when one must deploy or redeploy quickly, so train with both and make up your own mind. Note the long, narrow sand bag used in various pictures in this book. It is light, easy to carry, fast to position and very stable.

Prone bi-pod

Prone sling/bi-pod

Prone tri-pod

74

Prone tri-pod

Sandbag support

Sandbag barricade

Note use of a glove.

76

Kneeling supported, quick and useful

Sitting supported, very exposed

Standing supported

Strong side barricade

UNSUPPORTED

Unsupported shooting techniques require constant practice and are generally only used when absolutely **no other option** is available. It is essential that a sniper become familiar and competent with **sling shooting techniques** in all positions. The sling, with a little practice, can become a valuable stabilizing part of your weapons system. Learn to keep an even tension on the sling each time you shoot. Changes in sling tension can cause changes in bullet impact. Be sure the sling passes high around the upper arm but is not so tight that it restricts blood flow to the forearm or hand. You may be in position for a long period of time before being called on to shoot or relocate.

The sling and shooting jacket should add to your comfort as both are designed to hold the shooter in position with the **minimum** muscle tension required.

Study the following photographs carefully.

PRONE

The preferred of all unsupported positions. Lie directly behind or slightly off to the side of the weapon, whichever is most comfortable for you. Sometimes your location will force you to modify your normal position.

Keep the weapon as low as possible and avoid lifting the head too much and creating a strain on the neck. Breathe naturally and see if your reticle moves up and down, vertically, through your intended aiming point.

The stock should be **firmly** against the pad of the shoulder, not the bone. The cheek should also be placed **firmly** against the stock. Ensure the eye relief, distance from scope to eye, is correct **(about 3″-3½″)**. Prone position will put you a little closer to your scope than standing, so beware of getting "bitten" under recoil.

Prone sling

Single point sling

Double point sling

Note the elbow positioned under the weapon.

Prone without sling

81

KNEELING

A fast and versatile position allowing good mobility when needed. Again, be as comfortable as possible and **avoid bone contact** between elbow and knee. Study photos for high and low positions.

High kneeling with sling

Low kneeling with sling

Kneeling without sling

Low kneeling

83

SITTING

A slow position to get out of in a hurry but comfortable for long periods. If you can get your back against a wall or post it will greatly improve your stability and comfort.

Sling sitting

Sitting

Sling sitting

Sitting without sling

STANDING

The **least desirable** of all positions, especially with a 12-16 pound weapon system. If at all possible find a better position or at least a barricade support. You will find strong side barricade very good but weakside all but impossible, especially trying to keep the weapon off of the hard surface.

Snap shots from the port arm's ready position is a useful exercise in case you have to make a fast **defensive shot** while moving into position.

Where the standing position is used, keep the strong side elbow elevated parallel to the ground or higher.

Sling ready   *Sling standing*

Sling ready

Sling standing

Standing, no sling

NOTE:

In all positions ensure that the supporting arm and elbow are directly under the fore end of the weapon, and the supporting hand is not gripping the weapon too tightly. In fact many shooters prefer just to let the weapon rest in the hand without gripping.

A **hand stop,** attached to the fore end, will prevent the hand sliding forward. A **tight sling** will serve the same purpose. See photos.

Kneeling

Standing

Kneeling

19
SNIPER TRAINING

Sniper/counter sniper training does not require sophisticated or expensive equipment, just a suitable range and a little imagination.

All training should be based on the **ONE SHOT=ONE KILL** concept.

Maximum realism should be stressed throughout the training program.

HOW OFTEN

Some agencies train on a weekly or bi-weekly basis, even if it is just to shoot a few rounds. It has been proven that small amounts of regular training are more beneficial than infrequent sessions requiring many rounds.

The FBI policy of issuing the snipers their weapons, so that they are with them at all times, should be followed by all agencies. In this way the snipers can have access to their weapons and train whenever they get time.

You should test your weapon system at least four times a year, as the seasons and conditions change. But realistically most units will only train as a group **once a month.** The quarterly shoots can become the **documented** qualifications.

TRAINING

Begin each training session by logging a cold shot and a group at 100 yards. If zeroing must be done, do it at this point and log the changes. After the cold shot and group, try to make training varied and challenging.

Practice

- Known and unknown distance shooting. Learn to judge distance by object size as seen through your scope.
- All position shooting.
- Target identification exercises with group shot photographs or pictures from books and magazines.
- Shooting on command, within ½ second.
- Simultaneous shooting with other snipers. Communications become critical when coordinated fire is required.
- Exertion and shooting. Run the 100 yards from the target to your shooting position and shoot within 10 seconds of arrival.
- Night movement and shooting. Utilize natural and artificial light, static and strobe. Practice having the #2 sniper illuminate the target with a good flashlight and shooting instantly. This will work well out to 100 yards.

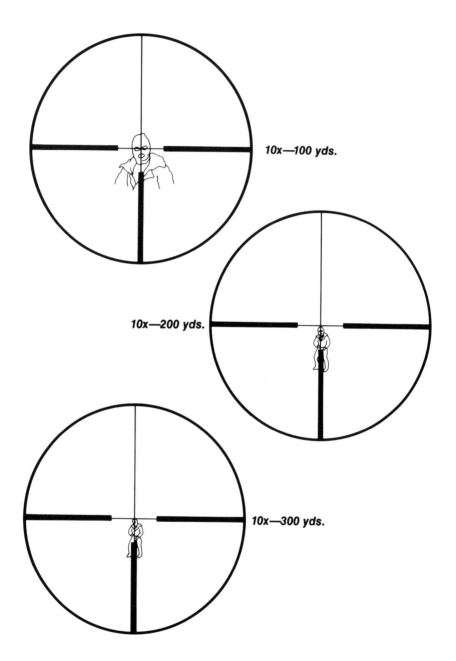

10x—100 yds.

10x—200 yds.

10x—300 yds.

Sniper weapon (.308 Win) is zeroed for 100 yds. At 200 yds. a 4½'' drop will produce a center head shot. At 300 yds. a 15''-16'' drop will produce a center chest shot. For military 500 meter zero see page 58.

- Cross training on other weapons. Log where the other snipers' weapons print in your hands.
- Bullet penetration and deflection tests. Use both regular and plate glass. Also car windshields, double glaze and safety glass.
- Moving and bobbing targets. A simple rope operated system is all that is needed but find a local range that has a variable speed mover as well. The turning type targets are also very useful for target identification shots.
- Close proximity barricade/hostage shots.

Do the bulk of your training at 100 yards or less but practice out to 300 yards as well. This would be the practical ranges for most police actions. Practice at longer ranges of 300 to 600 yards would be beneficial but not essential. Few ranges are set up for this type of shooting, so a call to your local military camp may be in order. This would also give you the opportunity to shoot alongside military snipers and learn the techniques of range estimation and reading the wind.

Wind is rarely a factor the law enforcement sniper has to contend with because of the short ranges he is asked to shoot at. Even at 200 yards, a **5-10mph** cross wind will only produce a 1"-2" bullet deflection, so at 100 yards it is negligible.

Learning to dope the wind is best learned by experience at long range rifle competitions. In fact, snipers should be encouraged to shoot any form of rifle competition which will put them under pressure and improve their skills.

WIND CHART

These are only approximations.

Wind ▸ ▾ Range	5mph	10mph	15mph	20mph
200m	1.2	2.4	3.6	4.8
300m	2.7	5.4	8.1	10.9
400m	4.8	9.6	14.4	19.2
500m	7.5	15.0	22.6	30.0
600m	11.0	21.0	32.0	43.0
1000m	30.0	60.0	90.0	120.0

All wind deflections represented in inches.

The above calculations are for a direct cross-wind. If the wind is at an angle, from the front or rear, to the path of the bullet, these figures can be halved.

Again, most law enforcement shots will be **under 90 yards** and protected from wind by buildings. The deflection is virtually non-existent.

GENTLE BREEZE   MODERATE BREEZE   STRONG WIND

Wind Indication

DRY FIRE

Dry fire is still one of the best forms of no-cost training. The scope will magnify your errors in breathing and trigger control, that you may not see under recoil.

Assume a shooting position, pick an aiming point and squeeze off a dry shot. Whichever way your reticle moves is where the shot would have gone.

We cannot over-emphasize the need to check and double check that the weapon is **unloaded.** No point in scaring the Chief as you track his car through the parking lot.

LOW COST TRAINING

Many individual snipers have gone out and purchased their own **.22 long rifles** and precision air rifles as a source of low cost indoor training. Set up similar to their primary sniper weapon, with a scope, they can get hours of training and amusement at home or on ranges where the heavier calibers are not permitted.

The lower velocities of an air rifle are very unforgiving and will help polish your technique and follow through.

Use small reduced size targets or pictures cut from magazines to add realism to this exercise.

SWAT TRAINING

In addition, the sniper must maintain all his regular SWAT skills, so attend all regular training sessions with the team, including handgun, building entry, search, rappelling and climbing, prisoner handling, arrest procedure, unarmed combat, helicopter deployment, distinguished visitor protection, etc.

Give the other team members the opportunity to see you shoot and to understand the precision of which you are capable. Remember that they will be moving out **in front** of your weapon during an assault or rescue.

TARGETS

Targets should also be varied and interesting. Following are a few examples of the targets we utilize.

Steel—at least one inch thick and hung on chains or counterweighted to reset automatically. A little smaller than head and chest size plates are used and definitely speed up training when targets do not have to be patched. The plates can be set as knock-downs but then it takes time to reset them.

Balloons—a good visual indication of a hit. Excellent for simultaneous shooting.

Clay birds as used for trap shooting, hung on the heads of targets.

Dummies—old department-store models are excellent for a three-dimensional effect.

Clothes—hang clothes, hats and wigs on targets for added realism.

Duel A Tron—good shoot/no shoot targets.

Photos—make your own hostage situation/terrorist scenes; that is what the technical division of your agency is for.

Sako .22 long rifle for inexpensive practice

NIGHT SHOOTING

Since many operations will begin or continue through the hours of darkness (average operation is 18-24 hours) special attention should be paid to **low and no light** training.

The scope sight magnifies not only the target but also available light. Practice shooting in early morning and late evening conditions. Set-up various artificial light conditions using car headlights, flashlights, flares, strobes and street lamps. Shoot with both back lighting and front lighting, observing that back light eliminates facial features.

If you have a good night scope it should be mounted on a separate weapon to avoid loss of zero in switching scopes. Do not expose a night scope to direct light and be sure to carry extra batteries for the unit.

Flashlight Method

Have the #2 sniper illuminate the target with a good Streamlite type flashlight. Out to 100 yards, with the added light gathering of the scope, it will be like daylight.

See **COMMUNICATIONS** in this book.

Use the count-down method for this:

5
4
3
2—#2 sniper illuminates target
1—#1 sniper fires

Immediately both snipers relocate to a new position. The muzzle flash and light would have compromised the initial location.

This is a technique that should be perfected during practice and training. It is also a lot cheaper than a $5,000 night scope.

Be sure the flashlight is held **forward** of the scope so that the sniper is not illuminated and the light does not reflect off the rear lens.

Radio controlled fire practice

Simulation of the night flashlight technique

Muzzle flash from a handgun at night. The rifle will be considerably less.

Rappel training

Prisoner handling tactic

96

MOVING TARGETS

The following data is supplied only as an example of how to develop your own data on engaging moving targets.

Everyone will get slightly different results because barrel length, caliber, muzzle velocity and ammunition are all variables in this exercise.

Using the **H&K PSG-1** and **Federal 168 grain** match ammo we found the following:

A target moving at 8'/second, **a fast jog,** at **50 yards** required a lead of approximately **6"** from the point of impact.

The same target at the same speed required 12"-14" at **100 yards.** Normal walking speed is about 4-5'/second, so halve these leads if the target is walking: 3"-4" at 50 yards and 6"-7" at 100 yards.

These were shot with the target moving directly across in front of our position. If the target is moving towards you or away at an angle, the leads can also be halved or modified in proportion to the angle of movement.

MATHEMATICAL APPROACH

D' = DISTANCE TO TARGET IN FEET
MV = MUZZLE VELOCITY IN FEET PER SECOND
TS = TARGET SPEED IN FEET PER SECOND

$$\frac{D'}{MV \times TS} = \text{LEAD IN FEET} \qquad \frac{300}{2400 \times 8} = 1 \text{ FOOT (12")}$$

confirms range results

TO CONVERT M.P.H. TO FEET/SECOND

MPH x 5280 and DIVIDE BY 3600

4 x 5280 = 21,120, ÷ 3600 = 5.8 feet per second (brisk walking speed)

The bottom line is that snipers must get out to the range and practice on moving targets to become proficient. Guesswork has no place in sniper training, especially when the target may have a hostage in tow. Only experience and a lot of practice will give you the feel for **SUCCESSFULLY** engaging moving targets.

When setting up your lead on a moving target, remember to move with the target and **follow through** after the shot. Skeet shooting can be a good training exercise for lead and follow through.

The **British** method is to pick a point ahead of the target and let the target move into it and fire. One can become very proficient at this method with a little practice.

Moving target shooting is one place where bi-pods are a hindrance. A sling prone position gives more freedom of movement.

Training on moving targets

Mover at 100 yards

Mover at 50 yards

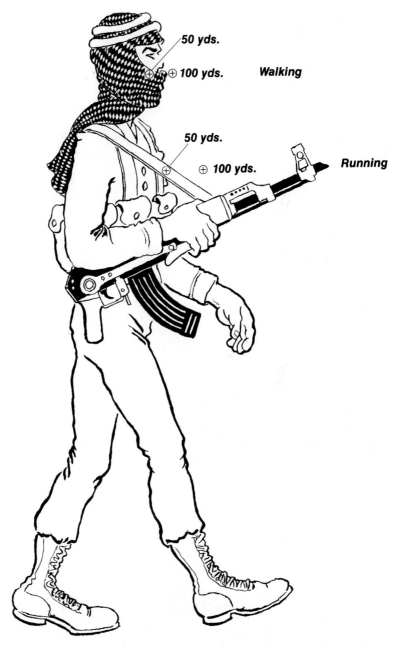

50 yds.

100 yds. *Walking*

50 yds.

100 yds. *Running*

Lead on a moving target at 50 and 100 yards

The sniper will supply cover for a casualty recovery team.

Sniper covers window during rappel assault and is prepared to engage any threats to the entry team.

20
PHYSICAL CONDITIONING

Even though every sniper considers himself a **"finely tuned, precision shooting machine"** he should not neglect his basic physical conditioning.

A sniper who is part of a Special Response Team should be expected to participate in all fitness programs and obstacle courses with the rest of the team.

In addition to team training, the sniper should have his own exercise routine designed to improve his shooting ability. The program will consist of two parts: **ANAEROBIC,** to improve arm and shoulder strength, which will aid in supporting his heavy weapons system and climbing, and **AEROBIC,** to improve heart and breathing rates. In order to shoot accurately one must be able to keep the heart rates slow and regular. This can only be achieved with adequate running, swimming, cycling or similar stamina exercises.

A **minimum** program would consist of one hour in the gym with weights, and 30-40 minutes running every second day. See our suggested program.

Good health and good physical condition will better help you control the stress and pressures of your job.

Keep sugars, fats and alcohol to a minimum. Even coffee can have an adverse effect on your shooting ability.

As a law enforcement officer, and even more as a sniper, you have a tremendous responsibility to yourself, your team and society to be the best that you can be. If you cannot make that commitment, ask to be reassigned.

Push-ups

SAMPLE FITNESS PROGRAM

Anaerobic

All these exercises are designed to increase shoulder and upper arm strength, to help support the heavy sniper rifle. If you are already on a balanced weight training program, then these exercises are probably included.

Do not go into an anaerobic program with the idea of bulking or building large muscles, but of developing muscle strength and stamina.

All exercises will be done in sets of five, using a decreasing number of repetitions.

Five sets of reps: 10, 10, 8, 8, 6.

If you do the five sets easily, increase the weight.

Do: BENCH PRESS, BARBELL (120+ lbs)
INCLINE BENCH, BARBELL (100+ lbs) or DUMBBELLS (30+ lbs)
FRONT THROWS, DUMBBELLS (25+ lbs)
STANDING FLYS, DUMBBELLS (25+ lbs)

Do: CURLS, WIDE GRIP, BARBELL (60+ lbs)
CURLS, DUMBBELLS (30+ lbs)
CURLS, CLOSE GRIP, BARBELL (60+ lbs)
BEHIND HEAD PRESS (FRENCH CURLS) (30+ lbs)
KICK BACKS, DUMBBELLS (25+ lbs)

Other useful exercises are CHIN UPS, PUSH UPS, SIT UPS and the illustrated rifle exercises.

Aerobic

RUN 4-5 MILES EVERY SECOND DAY
and/or CYCLE ONE HOUR OF HILLS AND FLAT
and/or SWIM 30-40 MINUTES

The object of aerobic exercise is to considerably increase the heart rate and keep it there for 20-40 minutes (generally above 120 beats per minute).

If time is short, then concentrate on your aerobic training. A strong and healthy cardiovascular system is far more important than big muscles.

If you "have to" drink beer and eat junk food, then be prepared to pay the price. Get out there and run it off the next morning.

Start position

Hold 20 seconds

Hold 20 seconds

Hold 10 seconds

Hold 20 seconds

Hold 10 seconds

Repeat this routine as many times as you wish, to develop upper arm and shoulder strength.

Wide grip curls

Seated curls

Front throws

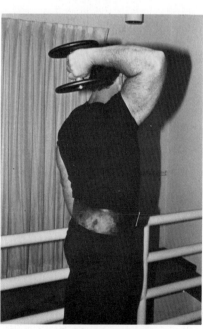

Behind-head press

Seated curls

Standing flys

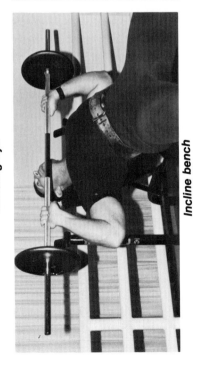

Kick-backs

Incline bench

106

21
STANDARDS AND QUALIFICATIONS

Apart from the ongoing evaluation of personnel throughout their training and operational career, shooting and fitness qualifications should be held on a regular basis **(every 3-4 months).** The sniper weapon system needs to be tested and zeroed quarterly, or as the seasons and conditions change, so this is an excellent time to include a documented qualification shoot.

Qualifications will help maintain the unit in a high state of readiness and should test both individual and team skills.

The following example is specifically for snipers.

INSPECTION
A full kit inspection to ensure that lost, damaged or worn equipment is replaced and all other gear is clean and functional. Pay special attention to weapons, night vision and communications equipment.

MARKSMANSHIP
All qualification results should be dated, signed and witnessed and given to your agency for legal record.
- Cold shot, prone supported at 100 yards, within 1″ of point of aim.
- 5-shot group, prone supported, 1″ at 100 yards.
- Any supported position at 100 yards. Center head shot (4″). This would include sitting, kneeling, standing or prone.

This would be a 10-round qualification course.

Additional tests
- Sprint 100 yards and then shoot consistent head shots at 100 yards, prone supported.
- Partial head shots (barricade/hostage situations) from any supported position, 50-100 yards. Shooting instantly on command to fire.
- 200 yards, center head (4″) from prone supported.
- 300 yards, center chest (6″) from prone supported.

NOTE:
A three-point Bench Rest stand and sand bags are very helpful for testing the weapon and eliminating human error.

PHYSICAL REQUIREMENTS
Run 2 miles in under 16 minutes
Pushups, 40-50 in 60 seconds
Situps, 50-60 in 60 seconds
Chin-ups, 10-plus

Also make maximum use of obstacle courses. Since each one is different you will have to establish your own minimum time.

Sit-ups

Running should be an essential part of a sniper's daily routine.

PART III

OPERATIONS

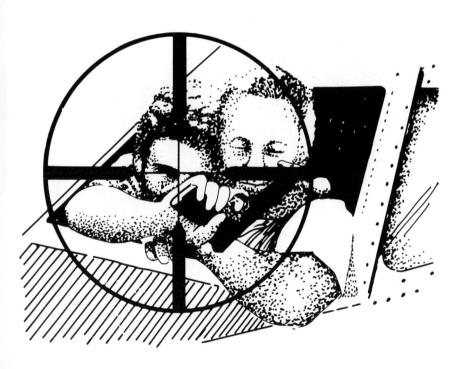

Simultaneous sniper fire requires excellent communications and timing. See pages 115 and 116.

22
COMMUNICATIONS

When human life is at stake, it is essential that your communications be **clear** and **accurate**.

The initial role of a sniper or sniper/observer, in a tactical operation, is to gain a good position of advantage and feed intelligence information back to the team leader or SWAT Commander. For this you must learn to speak calmly and clearly, utilizing good radio procedure. You should also practice describing structures, suspects and movement to your team leader so that you develop a feel for each other's methods.

BRIEFING

During the briefing, prior to operation, the sniper should learn his condition:

RED: DO NOT shoot under any circumstances.
YELLOW: Shoot in defense of life only.
GREEN: Shoot on sight.

The sniper should also receive a description of suspect(s) and hostage(s), and be given his codes and call signs.

OPERATIONS LOG

From the very start of an operation the #2 sniper should begin keeping an operational log of **all** communications traffic and commands. This would include sketches, descriptions, all reported movement of suspects, hostages, etc., all fire commands given by the CP and any intelligence information reported to the CP. This log will become an important document during the post-shooting investigation, so log times and dates as well.

TARGETING

Try to establish a **simple** system to bring the sniper or team leader on target.

A house has basically four sides:

> FRONT—WHITE
> BACK—BLACK
> LEFT—GREEN
> RIGHT—RED

The suspect house would be #1, the house to the left #2, the house behind #3 and to the right #4.

Motorola Expo system. Position radio for easy access to volume and channel controls.

#2 sniper handles communications and binoculars.

So movement on the left side of the suspect house would simply be transmitted as:

"MOVEMENT 1 GREEN"

Movement to the right of the house to the right of the suspect house would be:

"MOVEMENT 4 RED"

These codes can be established during the Briefing period.

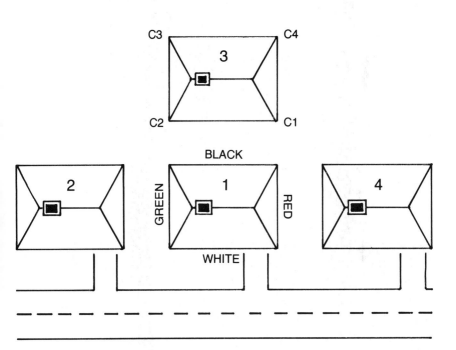

Residential codes–one possible method of labeling or identifying specific areas.

To bring the sniper's attention to a particular window on a highrise building, count your floors down from the top and the windows in from the left. So a transmission like:

"GTE 37"

would mean the GTE building down 3 floors and in from the left 7 windows. We count from the top for two reasons: (1) hostile snipers generally position themselves high in a building to maximize their advantage, and (2) to avoid the confusion of whether the ground floor or the first row of windows is the first floor. Also some buildings are built on sloping terrain so the downhill side may have one or two more floors.

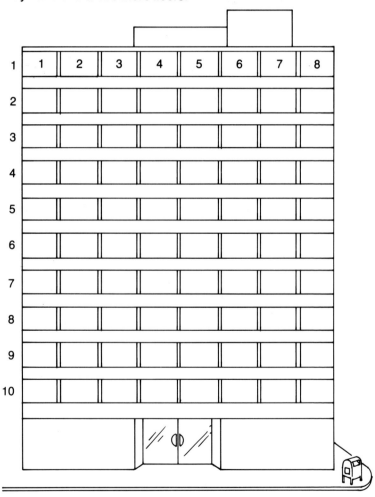

Window identification

In open areas use the **"clock-ray"** method, twelve being directly ahead of the sniper. So:

"10 O'CLOCK, 150"

would mean front left, 150 yards from the sniper's location.

When using a specific object as a reference point, use the object, the direction, then the distance. Example:

"BARN, LEFT, 100"

would mean left of the barn, 100 yards.

CALLING SHOTS

Whether training or operations, think of the target in terms of the face of a clock: 12 being top, 6 bottom, 9 left and 3 right.

Always call the clock direction first, then the distance. So a shot high and to the left may be **"11 o'clock, 7 inches"**. A miss low and to the right may be **"Miss, 5 o'clock, 3 feet"**. This is a procedure to be practiced by sniper and observer, especially important for long-range field operations.

SIMULTANEOUS SHOOTING

Shooting simultaneously with another sniper is a very important skill to develop, and requires much practice.

Prodecure as follows:

Team leader requests, **"Sniper status."**

Snipers respond by numbers, **"One on," "Two on," "Three off," "Four on."**

Team leader will respond with **"FIRE,"** or **"HOLD."**

If it is the Green Light, **"FIRE,"** all snipers will shoot simultaneously (within ¼ second).

Or the Team leader may indicate, **"One and four FIRE."**

All commands should be repeated twice, **"COMMAND FIRE, FIRE."**

After shooting the sniper will acknowledge, **"SHOT OUT."**

This is an exercise best practiced on balloons for a visual indication of simultaneous impact.

GREEN LIGHT

Some agencies are moving away from the Green Light concept and allowing officers to use normal discretion as law enforcement personnel. **DEFENSE OF LIFE.** Then as the problem develops they may be given the command, **"At the first clear opportunity,"** regardless of defense of life at that precise moment.

We have one big problem with this. The sniper is not in a position to see "the big picture." When he drops one terrorist, there may be another in a different location capable of killing other hostages. It is preferable to have your snipers under strict control and to engage **PRE-SELECTED TARGETS ONLY.** Defense of fellow team members, during the assault, would be the exception.

GREEN LIGHT COMMAND

Also known as the "Fire Command" will generally be given by the senior man in the CP. He may make the decision but then leave the command to the assault element team leader, so that it may be better coordinated with the rescue effort.

The actual command must be given twice, **"COMMAND FIRE, FIRE!"**, to avoid any misunderstanding. The controller may just be saying, "Wait for me to say 'Fire'," but when the sniper hears, ". . . fire" he may shoot.

During a **Continuous Green Light** the sniper will radio **"SHOT OUT"** after firing each time.

COUNT-DOWN SYSTEM

This is a verbal count-down by the CP or team leader.
For simultaneous fire:

5
4
3
2
1—all snipers fire immediately

Sniper initiated assault:

5
4
3—snipers fire
2—blast from stun grenades or breaching charge
1—assault team moves in

Night shot:

5
4
3
2—lights on target
1—snipers fire
Snipers #1 & #2 immediately relocate after muzzle flash.

Window Shot:

5
4
3
2—first sniper fires and breaks glass
1—second sniper engages target

FINAL NOTE:

It cannot be over-stressed the importance of clear communications between the team leader, snipers and observers.

Select a high quality, hands-free system like the **Motorola Expos, MTs or MXs.** If you can run your snipers on a separate frequency, all the better, but remember to keep them updated on all developments. If you are using a scrambler system your transmissions will become very garbled if you try to speak fast.

Some agencies have even gone to a hard wire light system to initiate sniper fire, because of communication problems. This visual command system seems less disturbing to the sniper as well.

Note hands-free communication system used by German GSG-9.

Helicopter deployment

Israeli sniper

23
TACTICS AND DEPLOYMENT

STAND-BY STATUS

This is an important and often neglected part of SWAT procedure that will have a significant influence on your response time and effectiveness as a sniper.

All equipment should be yours personally or permanently assigned to you by the agency; there is no time for requisition forms or unnecessary bureaucracy.

Weapons should be zeroed and cleaned, log books up to date, packs and go-boxes checked and inventoried on a regular basis. Ensure that consumables and worn equipment are replaced promptly.

CALL-OUT

Upon call-out to a developing situation, suiting up and equipment checks should be done quickly, carefully and quietly, either at base or on sight prior to briefing. Remember to check your partner's gear for noise and reflection. This is also the time to run a dry patch through the barrel of your weapon to remove any surplus oil or foreign matter.

WEAPONS CHECK

Ensure scope adjustment knobs and bullet drop compensators are correctly set; confirm scope zero with collimator; check position or tension on action mounting bolts; check for contact points between barrel and fore end; check scope mounting bolts for position or movement; be sure you have the correct ammunition from the same lot number used to zero the weapon.

CAMOUFLAGE

Camouflage must be matched to the terrain in which you expect to be deployed. If your jurisdiction includes both city and rural areas you will probably need two sets of gear: jungle or desert fatigues for the rural areas and grey/black or dark blue for the urban areas.

Pay careful attention to weapons and other specialized equipment that may give off **noise** or **reflection.** Anything attached to the barrel and fore-end of your weapon may upset the zero.

Agencies required to operate in the colder regions will also need to consider the use of warm, thermal uniforms and a white over-shell.

The most important part of camouflage is to darken and break up the exposed skin on your face and hands either with mask and gloves or paint stick. See photos.

The basic principles of concealment are:

- LIGHT—avoid using a flashlight, striking matches or smoking in position. Set your pack and equipment so it can be easily found in the dark.
- NOISE—nothing will give your position away faster than unnecessary noise, especially metallic sounds.
- MOVEMENT—movement attracts attention, keep it to a minimum once you are in position.
- SHAPE—a good example is a sniper silhouetted on a roof-line.
- REFLECTION—flashes from polished metal, lenses or high gloss stocks.
- COLOR—avoid light colors at night or moving on a light background in a dark uniform. Try to match your uniform to your area of operation.
- SMELL—to a lesser degree but you would be amazed how many weapons reek of solvent and oil.

Carefully consider all of the above when preparing your personal weapons and equipment.

Note exposed face and hands.

Effective use of a sniper veil.

Field camouflage

Urban camouflage

Keep basic equipment light and simple. Extra equipment can be carried in a back-pack. Medium threat ballistics vest worn under the shooting jacket.

Note the glare from this barrel.

BRIEFING

At the briefing all equipment should be secure so that your full attention can be given to the team leaders and advisors. Listen carefully and be prepared to take notes. If you have doubts or questions ask them now—it will be too late when you are deployed on a roof some distance away.

Do not allow yourself to be rushed too much; it is important that you go into the operation knowing that you and your equipment are squared away.

Listen carefully for suspect and hostage descriptions **(PHOTOS CAN BE A BIG HELP),** expected team movement and your fire control status **(RED YELLOW GREEN).**

If the team leader and the snipers have matching diagrams of the location it will help tremendously with targeting and radio communication. Certain locations can be labelled numerically or alphabetically for better radio security.

STOCKHOLM SYNDROME

This is a problem that can affect a sniper required to watch a suspect for long periods through a powerful scope.

Limit the amount of information the sniper is given about the suspect during the briefing period. Especially personal information that has no impact on the tactical facets of the operation.

The syndrome can manifest itself by the sniper developing sympathies and feelings toward the suspect, caused by long periods of very close observation.

A sniper must almost psych himself in the opposite direction to combat this.

POST BRIEFING

At this point you may want to make last-minute additions or changes to your basic load. The briefing will have given you a better indication of what will be expected of the snipers on this operation. Deploy to your assigned or selected location as soon as possible; the team will be awaiting your observations and intelligence.

At night and in darkened buildings avoid running. To trip and fall now may injure yourself or damage your weapons system. A bruised or scraped body will not help your concentration in the hours ahead, so move quickly, quietly and carefully.

BRIEFING SYSTEM

For many years the military has used a simple system to remember the briefing sequence, S. M. E. A. C.:

SITUATION—current status, number of hostages/hostage takers, weapons involved, shots fired, prior histories, an overview of the situation to date.

MISSION—the role of the sniper and assault elements in this operation. Final aim.

EXECUTION—the actual mechanics of how the operation will go down. Detailed description of each man's assignment, sniper locations, rescue team jump-off point and perimeter security. Possible evacuation plan.

ADMIN AND LOGISTICS—equipment required, where to get it, shift changes and food supply. Medical assistance if necessary. Post operation prisoner search and movement.

COMMAND AND SIGNALS—who is in charge, chain of command, codes, fire control orders, contingency plans.

Use diagrams, plans and photos as much as possible. Ensure that every man has a clear picture of his role in relation to the team effort. Have team members repeat their assignments back to you to reinforce the information. Allow time for questions.

Leave the plan flexible enough to be modified as the intelligence flows back to the CP. Do not close your ears to outside input; you are dealing with a dynamic and unpredictable situation.

DEPLOYMENT

Snipers should always be deployed in a two-to-one ratio against hostile suspects. This was a lesson well learned after the **Munich Olympic Massacre.** A counter terrorist team must have firepower superiority so, to this end, some teams train all their members as snipers with assigned rifles.

Sniper teams should also be deployed at **right angles** to possible suspect movement. This way, whether the hostage is to the front or side of the hostage taker, one of the teams will always have a clear shot. See diagram.

Another advantage of two snipers shooting simultaneously is that the burden of responsibility is now shared, thus taking the pressure off a lone sniper.

Snipers should deploy, relocate and leave the area of operation in a low key manner. The sniper(s) should be the best kept secret in a tactical situation. If the terrorist/criminal indicates that he/she is aware of their location, relocate them immediately.

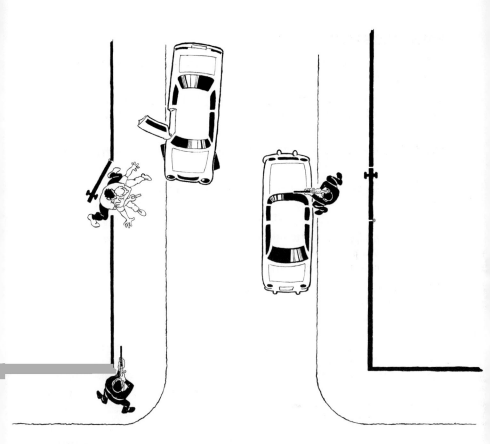

MOVEMENT

Since the sniper will be deploying with a heavy, bolt-action weapon it is best if the sniper/observer cover their movements with a semi-automatic weapon.

Avoid open or lighted areas but if that is not possible move through them quickly and quietly. Select the next available cover before moving out. Study the terrain for obstacles that may trip or hinder your movement.

When climbing on the outside of structures be sure to have adequate cover fire if necessary. Do not over-extend your climbing ability. Use ropes on steep-pitch roofs. Often you will be deploying in already secured buildings on the perimeter of the operation; try to respect the occupants' personal property.

If forced entry is required see the chapters in **"S.T.T.U. SWAT TACTICS"** on **"Entry and Movement."** Be particularly careful on stairwells and be conscious of interior lighting.

Where an extended rooftop deployment is expected, set up a lift rope behind the building to pass up additional food and equipment. This is something the sniper/observer should handle.

WEAPONS SAFETY

Normally, it should not be necessary for the sniper to run or climb with a chambered weapon, especially if it is slung on his back. The sniper should have an observer covering his movement.

The only time the weapon would be **chambered during movement** is if the sniper has the weapon in **both** hands and there is **imminent danger.**

The actual mechanical safety on the weapon should be regularly tested during training but never trusted 100%. There is no substitute for **safe** gun handling, **muzzle control** and keeping your finger **away from the trigger.**

When the sniper is deployed in an observation mode or the assault/rescue element is moving in front of his location or line of sight, it is best to elevate the weapon and observe through the lower quadrants of the scope. This is to avoid placing the cross-hairs on someone he **does not** intend to harm. Secondly, it is best to raise the bolt handle so that the weapon cannot be fired accidentally. This is not opening the bolt but simply leaving the thumb draped over the bolt handle so that a small movement will bring the weapon back into "fire ready." If the weapon is semi-automatic, there is no alternative but to use the safey and be very **muzzle conscious.**

Note thumb on bolt in safe/ready position.

NIGHT VISION

The rifle scope or binoculars can be of tremendous help in improving your night vision capability, but it will be helpful to also understand the basic principles of night vision.

- Give your eyes time to adapt to the conditions, 30 minutes.
- Use off-center vision. When looking directly at an object, the image is formed on the cone region of the eye which is not sensitive at night. When looking slightly to the side of an object, the image is formed on the area of the retina containing rod cells which are sensitive in darkness.
- Protect your night vision. Bright light will destroy your night vision, so close one eye and preserve partial night sight until you have time to readjust.
- Vitamin A is important to night vision. Colds, headaches, fatigue, narcotics, heavy smoking and alcohol reduce the ability to see at night.
- Be confident, trust your eyes.

126

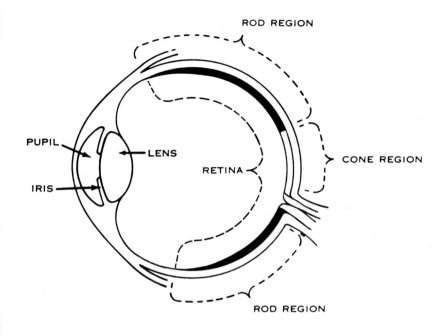

ROD REGION

CONE REGION

ROD REGION

PUPIL

LENS

IRIS

RETINA

Snipers protect riot control team and emergency services personnel.

24
LOCATION SELECTION

The sniper, being a highly trained specialist, should be the most qualified to select a sniper location. He will be aware of the locations that will give him the greatest tactical advantage for both observation and effective fire on selected targets.

CONDITIONS TO CONSIDER

- Range: stay within 100-200 yards. Generally less.
- Field of view/area of domination
- Cover and concealment: cover stops bullets, concealment does not.
- Weather conditions: from hot sun to snowfall.
- Movement of rescue team: can you effectively cover them?
- Wind direction if gas deployed: do you have a mask?
- Angle of shot through glass windows: possible deflection.
- Mobility: for fast relocation, suspect movement or fire danger.
- Comfort: you may be there a long time.
- Lighting: artificial and natural, day to night.
- Security: from rear attack or the News Media.

The average operation lasts **18-24 hours.** Automatically select second and third locations in advance.

Be aware of the locations of your fellow snipers and perimeter personnel, to avoid dangerous cross fire. Selecting positions above the suspect location will usually prevent this.

Avoid **silhouetting** yourself on **roof lines** at all costs, especially when you could set-up inside a window. What you sacrifice in field of view you will gain in concealment. Some snipers have even gone to the trouble of cutting "mouse or loop holes" in walls to gain the best position:

Deploying diagonally on the corners of a building is fine for observers but not for a sniper. The sniper needs to be able to see in windows and if the shot is called for, shoot at as close to a 90-degree angle as possible, to avoid bullet deflection through glass.

Be prepared to maintain your position for long periods. Hopefully you will be working as a **two-man team** and can switch out to relieve eye fatigue, cramp and the calls of nature.

If you are alone in a critical position be prepared to get hungry, thirsty, cold, hot, wet, tired, bored, forgotten, eaten by insects, sunburned, cramped and if necessary even to urinate in your pants.

129

A tower top sniper can be very dangerous to both civilians and police response teams.

SPECIAL NOTE:

Do not assume that your distance from the suspect will protect you from his **"reaching out and touching YOU."**

Make maximum use of **cover,** to stop bullets, not just **concealment.** With the type of weapons available today, it is not inconceivable that the villains may have the weapons and optics to hit you at any distance. It has happened already!!

Sand bags, even if you use a bi-pod, are very comforting to have between you and the suspect location.

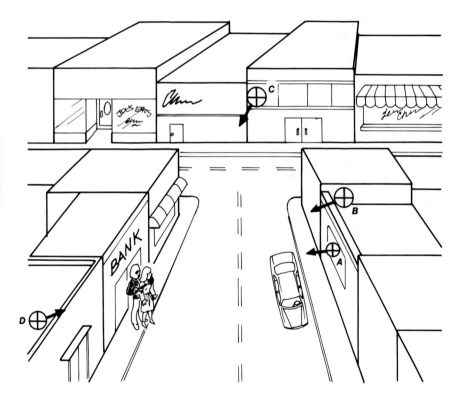

Position at least two snipers at right angles to each other. A and B would take the interior shot while C and D would take an exterior shot if A and B were blocked by a hostage. D could cover the rear of the bank if necessary.

Poor use of a car

Good use of the wheel and engine block for cover.

Visible from suspect location

Poor location

Better concealment

Correct **Incorrect**

Field craft should teach the correct use of cover and concealment. Take time to pre-select alternative locations early in the operation.

Use of a sandbag

Poor choice

Avoid roof lines

Good roof location

T.V. rest

Ironing board

Poor concealment

Hasty rest on a chair

Checking line of fire and selecting positions for a quick relocation.

Inside position. Note the use of a "Second Chance Command JAC."

The business end

Use of extended bi-pod. Very exposed.

Cover under vehicles is far from ideal.

Should move further into the trees for better concealment.

25
INTELLIGENCE

Two of the prime pieces of information the team will want from you are structural descriptions and suspect descriptions.

From your position note the types of doors, which way they swing, types and placement of locks, normal or plate glass windows, which ones are open, are there iron bars, can the team move quietly on the roof, are the drapes drawn or anything else that may be of tactical consideration.

As for the suspect(s), physical description, clothing, weapons, movement, calm or agitated, which windows are they using for observation points, etc.

The rescue team will also be interested in hostage locations and descriptions. Do not assume that everyone can see what you can see; when in doubt report it.

Given time, someone may be able to locate the building superintendent or builders to tell you exactly what type of glass was used in the windows you may have to shoot through.

FBI tries to deploy their teams with a camera and suitable telephoto/zoom lens. With **one-hour developing** this can be an excellent tool for passing around intelligence information. The zoom makes a good observation scope as well.

Remember to **record** all observations, communications traffic and CP commands. Date and time all records.

You are now ready to make **"the shot,"** if called upon, or continue to be a valuable observer and source of security to the rescue team or negotiators.

REQUISITES FOR SNIPER OPTION

Before the sniper is given the order to fire there are a few other tactical considerations. They are:

- At least two snipers for each target/suspect
- Assault/rescue team is ready for immediate follow-up
- Negotiators have secured the release of as many hostages as possible
- The perimeter security is complete and all exits and entrances are covered
- Innocent by-standers have been cleared from surrounding area
- All possible intelligence for the assault team has been collected and studied
- Snipers are confident in their ability to succeed
- Targets are positively identified

- Assume that there will only be one opportunity and **one shot.**

Now, if the situation warrants a lethal termination, the commander has covered all foreseeable requirements.

CRITICAL SITUATIONS

The following are just some of the situations in which an operational commander may be justified in authorizing the use of deadly force (sniper and/or assault option).

1. One or more hostages have already been killed.
2. Suspect has a prior history of killing.
3. Suspect shows willingness to kill.
4. Suspect is mentally unstable and capable of killing.
5. Terrorists using suicidal tactics.
6. Ideological reasons to kill and gain media attention.
7. Long-term psychological damage to hostages.
8. Immediate danger to hostages in need of medical attention.
9. Immediate danger to the community (water or power supply, rush hour traffic about to begin or school children in area).
10. Barricade suspect is preventing emergency personnel from performing their duties, e.g., fire, ambulance, gas, etc.
11. Effective counter measures to negotiation; makes demands, sets deadline, then breaks all contact.
12. Even though most situations will be negotiated, the longer it continues the less effective the law enforcement effort will appear.

THE HARDEST DECISION A COMMANDER WILL EVER HAVE TO MAKE IS WHETHER TO TAKE THE TACTICAL OPTION OR RISK THE SITUATION DETERIORATING FURTHER. Only an overt act of killing on the part of the hostage taker will make this decision easier.

26
DIGNITARY PROTECTION DETAIL

Up to this point we have covered the major considerations for sniper deployment on an operational call-out; criminal/terrorist barricade or hostage situation. Another assignment a law enforcement sniper may draw is a dignitary protection detail.

ROLE

To gain a high point and observe and report on movement on roof tops, in windows or in the gathering crowd.

To identify possible threats to the dignitary.

To report on movement seen by the close protection team on the ground or in the surrounding buildings.

To deny hostile snipers access to the roof tops.

To shoot upon armed attackers outside of the reach of the close protection team.

To neutralize roof top or window snipers.

To disable possible suicide drivers and vehicles.

DEPLOYMENT

The sniper may be required to deploy somewhere along the planned motorcade route or overlooking the site of a particular function or ceremony. Had snipers been deployed above the review stand when **Sadat** was assassinated in **Egypt,** they could have well saved his life from the terrorists in the military procession.

Secret Service Counter Sniper Teams habitually move ahead and with the President to protect against just such an incident. Political events often occur in wide open areas where long-range weapons and powerful scopes are essential.

Think like an assassin or hostile sniper but select a position not where he would, but where you can observe that location.

You may also be required to set-up above a courthouse to protect an arriving key witness from retaliation by underworld or drug related hit men.

ADVANCE WORK

Arrive early and give yourself time to study the location. Be more concerned with high-rise buildings that have **opening windows** than the newer ones that are totally air-conditioned and sealed.

Talk to the **Advance Cover Team** and find out what security procedures they have initiated. Make sure that they are well aware of your selected location and all team members are informed. Check that you can access or monitor their radio frequencies and in turn they can contact you when necessary.

If it is a long motorcade route that cannot be completely covered by counter snipers, select locations where the dignitary is most vulnerable; where the cars **slow down** for curves or intersections, the **loading and unloading** points, and the areas where the **crowd and news media** are the thickest.

RESEARCH

Study any past incidents where snipers or riflemen played a role in the assassination or attempted assassination of a dignitary. The **Kennedy** and **Sadat** incidents are classic examples.

Sadat might well have survived the assassination if the review stand and parade had been covered by an alert C.A.T. team.

*Position early enough
to observe all crowd movement.*

*Pay special attention
to open windows.*

Police sniper covers royal visit to Belfast, Ireland.

27
THE SHOT

The sniper's purpose in shooting is to stop **WITH CERTAINTY** the dangerous, or potentially dangerous, activity of the suspect. He **SHOOTS TO KILL WITH THE FIRST ROUND.**

Few law enforcement snipers are ever called upon to make the shot, but if your day comes there should be no doubt in your mind that you are capable of pulling that trigger. If you do have more than the normal worries or doubts discuss them with your team leader and consider reassignment.

MENTAL CONDITIONING

Maintain a **positive** mental attitude that in making the shot it is justified and in **defense of life.** You may not be terminating an assailant in the act but one that is capable of great harm if permitted to continue on his or her course of action.

Try to be impersonal in your regard for the **"target."** What you may have to do is simply a surgical action to remove a very dangerous cancer to society.

Do not expect or request **unnecessary** details about the suspect. The less you know about the target's personal life the less chance there is of becoming a victim to **Stockholm Syndrome** (developing sympathies for the target).

Some snipers **mentally** develop an animosity toward the potential target so that there will be no hesitation when the shot is called for. This is very easy when the suspect has already killed or maimed, as in the **McDonald's** incident in San Ysidro.

Do not identify the barricaded suspect or hostage taker by his or her **clothing;** he or she may have exchanged clothes with a hostage. You will want to be able to distinguish **facial features** before you make the shot.

SHOT PLACEMENT

The object of the shot is to terminate all body function as quickly as possible. **ONE SHOT STOP.** This is best achieved by hitting the central nervous system rather than the circulatory (heart/blood) or respiratory system (lungs) — but these may be the only secondary targets available to you.

Try to think in terms of **CENTER OF MASS** to the head. The traumatic shock to the skull cavity alone should prove lethal.

Other considerations are distance, angle, hostage proximity, possible bullet deflection and target movement. When reporting to the team leader be honest in your evaluation of whether you can guarantee the shot. Longer shots **(200 yards+)** should be to the body, while closer shots will be to the head or spine.

The shots shown in this book are the ideal but sometimes very difficult because of suspect movement, concealment or agitation. Keep in mind that an expanding, fragmenting rifle bullet, travelling at 2000+ feet per second, will only have to be within **2-3 inches** of these key spots to have an extremely high probability of ending the incident. Train hard and develop the confidence to find that elusive shot.

When in doubt about hitting the head, or if you are at all nervous, **do not hesitate** to take the body shot.

Do not attempt a shot if a hostage, bystander or team member is **directly behind** the target. The chance of total penetration is too great with a rifle.

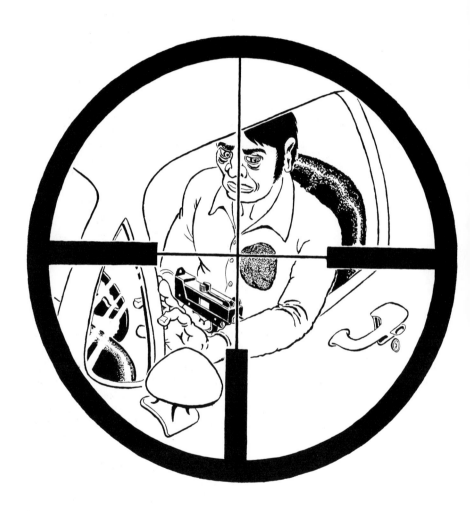

148

NEGOTIATORS

It is questionable whether a negotiator should be told that he is being used to draw a dangerous suspect into a suitable position for sniper take-down. Some negotiators have openly said they would rather not know, the danger being that over a long period of negotiation the negotiator may have built some personal bond with the criminal or terrorist. When told that he is to assist in a **tactical option,** the concern for the suspect may become evident in his voice or increased efforts to bring a quick, negotiated solution to the stand-off.

An **overt** display of sniper teams can be used as a bargaining point by the negotiator. When the suspect demands the snipers' withdrawal, simply relocate to a better, more **covert** position.

If the negotiator goes face to face with the suspect, the sniper should be on a very high state of readiness to make the shot. If the sniper cannot hear what is being said he should watch for **sudden changes** in the suspect's mood or **movement for a weapon.**

A trusted tactical negotiator may choose to pre-arrange hand signals or gestures to indicate that negotiation is hopeless and the sniper should take the shot. Be sure that this is a **command decision** from the CP or team leader.

POST SHOT PROCEDURE

After making the shot, come right back on target and prepare for **follow-up shots.** If there is any doubt about the effectiveness of your first shot, deliver an immediate second shot, especially if hostages or rescue team members are within the suspect's sphere of danger.

Watch how your target falls for an indication of the effectiveness of your head shot. If he goes limp and falls straight down or pitches forward, there is a very high probability that the shot was instantly fatal. If he falls to the side you have likely only partially incapacitated him. The only time you will sometimes see the suspect thrown back or back-flip is if he is hit center chest. Any experienced hunter will have seen this phenomenon.

Be sure to communicate "Shot out," and the target's reaction, to the Command Post immediately after firing—a task best performed by the SO or #2 sniper.

THE ASSAULT

The assault team should follow up the shot **immediately** to ensure target neutralization and secure the safety of the hostages. The sniper should stay on target and in position until the total conclusion of the operation. He should continue to observe and report on team and suspect movements, and supply cover fire as necessary to protect the team or the hostages.

If the situation becomes dynamic the sniper should be ready to relocate to a more advantageous position.

Some snipers prefer to go down and see the results of their work, others prefer to leave that to the crime scene people and try to remain on an **impersonal** level.

As soon as possible write your report, logging **all** relevant equipment and ballistic information while it is fresh in your mind. Your weapons log and operational log will now become very important documents.

Stay calm and talk **only** to your commander or the assigned investigation team. Avoid the locker room talk and the press until the investigation is completed. (The agency and other team members should do all in their power to maintain the anonymity of the sniper to protect him and his family from unnecessary social and Media pressure.)

The whole situation will become very tiring for both the sniper and his family. Expect to lose some sleep; that is normal.

Openly discuss your thoughts and feelings with your agency psychologist; he can be of great help at this time. Do not make the mistake of blocking out your family or resorting to alcohol.

Volumes have been written on post-shooting trauma, so I will leave that to the experts.

28
CONCLUSION

The selection, training and deployment of a sniper within a tactical element is a very involved and complex task. The following are a few essential points to keep in mind:

1. **Select the snipers carefully.**
2. **Select time-proven, quality weapon systems and equipment.**
3. **The sniper weapon should be permanently assigned to the sniper.**
4. **Seek out professional instruction and advice.**
5. **Train and qualify on a regular basis.**
6. **Keep training realistic and varied.**
7. **Train both as an individual and as a team.**
8. **Team leaders should make maximum use of a sniper's skills in observation and intelligence gathering.**
9. **Deploy snipers in a low-key manner.**
10. **Snipers should always seek cover over concealment.**
11. **Communicate clearly and log all commands, movement and observations.**
12. **The sniper should shoot only at pre-selected targets and on command from the CP.**
13. **The assault/rescue team should move in immediately after the shot.**
14. **The agency should do all in its power to protect the sniper and his family from the press after a shooting.**

Final note:

It is beyond the scope of any book to supply all the technical information relating to sniper weapons, all the current training methods in use around the world or all the tactical options open to a sniper in a dynamic and unpredictable operation.

It is the author's hope that we have at least supplied sufficient information to get an individual sniper or agency moving in the right direction.

As criminal and terrorist tactics change we must also change our methods and equipment to counter their threat. In future editions of this book we will try to bring you updated material in this field.

If our readers believe that they have current material related to sniper/countersniper in a law enforcement role, please do not hesitate to forward it to us for inclusion in future editions of SNIPER/COUNTERSNIPER.

Example of an S.T.T.U training target

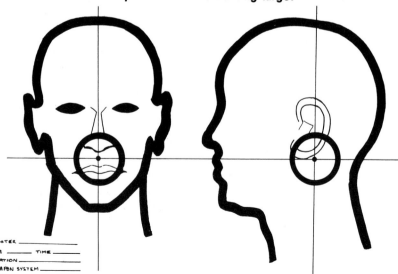

SHOOTER _____

DATE _____ TIME _____

LOCATION _____

WEAPON SYSTEM _____

AMMO. _____

LIGHT _____ WIND _____

DOPE CHANGE _____

SPECIAL EQUIPT. _____

HIGGINS

S.B.S.D.

GLOSSARY

ACRAGLASS—bedding compound made by Brownells

ACTION—mechanism of a weapon by which it is loaded, locked and fired

AMMO—ammunition

ANVIL— a fixed metallic point against which the priming compound is crushed and thereby detonated

AO—adjustable objective

AOS—Armed Offenders Squad

AP—armored piercing

ART—adjustable ranging telescope

ATS—Anti-Terrorist Squad

BALL—full jacketed bullet

BALLISTICS—the study of projectiles in motion

BARREL—tubular section of a weapon that guides the bullet during the rapid expansion of gases prior to exiting the muzzle

BASE—attachment for scope rings; can be one or two piece

BASR—Bolt Action Sniper Rifle

BEDDING—a manner in which the barrel and action are fitted to the stock

BENCH REST—competition shot over a solid table in search of ultimate accuracy

BERDAN PRIMER—early form of primer with no integral anvil, generally not reloadable

BI-POD—two-point rifle support

BOAT TAIL—bullet with tapered base

BOLT—moving section of the action

BOLT ACTION—a weapon that is manually reloaded by use of a bolt

BORE—inside of the barrel through which the bullet travels

BOXER—standard American type of primer

BRASS—empty cartridge case

BREECH—the loading end of the barrel

BULLET—missile or projectile

CALIBER—interior diameter of the barrel

CASE—container which holds all the components of a round of ammunition

CAT—Counter Attack Team

CENTER FIRE—centrally located primer in base of metallic cartridge.

CHAMBER—part of the bore, at the breech, formed to accept and support the cartridge

CHANNEL—groove cut in fore end of stock to accept barrel

CHRONOGRAPH—an instrument used to measure the velocity of a projectile

CLICKS—units of measure used in scope adjustment

COLD SHOT—the first shot from an un-fired weapon

COLLIMATOR—bore sighting device

CP—command post

CREEP—movement in trigger prior to discharge

CRIMP—bending inward of the mouth of the case in order to grip the bullet

CROSS HAIR—thin crossed lines used as an aiming device inside a scope

CROWN—machining of the muzzle end of the barrel

CST—Counter Sniper Team

DEFLECTION—change in path of the bullet due to wind or passing through a medium

DELTA—U.S. Counter Terrorist Team

DRIFT—the deviation of a projectile from the line of departure due to rotation or wind

DROP—the distance a projectile falls due to gravity measured from the line of departure

DROP COMPENSATOR—a sight adjustment to correct for bullet drop at various distances

DRY FIRE—aiming and firing the weapon without live ammunition

DUPLEX—wide posts converging in a fine cross hair, the ideal sniper reticle

ELEVATION—a vertical adjustment of a scope

EPOXY—two-part chemical compound which hardens when mixed

EXTERIOR BALLISTICS—the study of a projectile's flight after exiting the muzzle

EXTRACTOR—hook to remove cartridge from chamber

EYE RELIEF—distance from the shooter's eye to the rear of the scope

FACTORY LOAD—commercially manufactured ammunition

FBI—Federal Bureau of Investigation

FIRING PIN—part of a weapons mechanism that strikes the primer

FLOATING—removing all contact points between barrel and stock

FMJ—full metal jacket

FOULING—build-up of copper and powder residue in the bore

FORE END—forward section of the stock used for weapon support

FULL BORE—center fire competition, usually 7.62mm or over

GIGN—Groupe d'Intervention de la Gendarmerie Nationale

GRAIN—a unit of weight measure; 437.5 grains equal one ounce

GREEN LIGHT—authorization to fire

GROOVES—low points of rifling within a barrel

GROUP—the pattern made, at the target, of a number of shots fired with the same aiming point

GSG9—West German Counter Terrorist Team attached to border police

HAND LOAD—also called reload; hand manufactured ammunition

HAND STOP—device attached to weapon fore end to prevent hand sliding forward

HEAD SPACE—distance from the shoulder of the chamber to the face of the bolt in a closed position (method of measurement will vary with different calibers). A dimension critical to the safety of the shooter.

HOLD OFF—the distance aimed to the right or left of the target to compensate for wind or deflection

HOLD OVER—distance aimed above target to compensate for bullet drop

HOLD UNDER—distance aimed below target to compensate for a rising projectile

HOLLOW POINT—bullet with hollow cavity in the tip

HRT—Hostage Rescue Team (FBI)

INLETTING—removing of wood from inside of the stock to fit the barrel and action

INTERIOR BALLISTICS—the study of forces operating prior to the bullet exiting the muzzle

JACKET—copper covering over lead core of the bullet

KENTUCKY WINDAGE—term for guessing hold off on target

LANDS—high points in rifling of barrel

LOG—a detailed record of weapon's life

LOOP HOLE—hole cut to conceal sniper but allow shooting

LUBRICANT—substance to preserve metal and reduce friction

MAGAZINE—separate or integral part of a weapon which contains additional ammunition ready to fire

METALLIC SILHOUETTE—competition involving the knocking over of metallic animals at various ranges

MID-RANGE TRAJECTORY—the highest vertical distance of a bullet above the line of sight at a point approximately half-way from the muzzle to the target

MIL-DOT—popular form of sniper scope reticle

MINUTE-OF-ANGLE—a unit of angular measurement approximated as one inch to 100 yards (actually equal to 1.047″ per 100 yards)

MISFIRE—a round that fails to fire when struck by the firing pin

MOA—minute of angle

MOUNTS—refers to rings and bases for scope installation

MTU—Marksmen Training Unit

MUZZLE—the point at which the projectile leaves the barrel

MUZZLE VELOCITY—the speed of the bullet as it departs the weapon

NECK—portion of a cartridge case which grips the bullet

NO-SHOOT TARGET—hostage or bystander target used in training

NRA—National Rifle Association

PARALLAX—optical error caused by a change in the sniper's position in relation to the scope

PATCH—small piece of cloth used to clean bore

PILLAR BEDDING—form of bedding where the action mounting bolt holes are enlarged and sleeved with bedding compound

POA—point of aim

POINT OF AIM—point on the target where the cross hairs are positioned

POINT OF IMPACT—the point where the bullet strikes the target

POWDER—propellant material used in most firearms

PRIMER—small cup filled with detonating mixture which is used to ignite the propellant powder

PRIMER POCKET—recess in the base of the cartridge to accept the primer

PROJECTILE—bullet or missile in flight

PRONE—shooting position where shooter is lying flat

RAIL—adjustable insert in fore end of weapon to accept hand stop or sling

RANGE FINDER—system within a scope designed to estimate range of target

RECOIL—the backward thrust or kick caused by the discharge of a weapon

RECOIL LUG—heavy metal protrusion beneath the front of the action to transfer recoil to the stock

RECOIL PAD—rubber pad attached to rear of stock to protect shooter's shoulder and prevent slippage

RELEASE AGENT—coating used on all metal parts to prevent bedding compound adhering to the barrel and action

RELOAD—hand loaded ammunition

RETICLE—the sighting device within a scope

RETINA—light sensitive layer at the back of the eye

RIFLE—a long weapon with a grooved bore designed to make the bullet spin

RIFLING—the grooves within the barrel designed to spin the bullet and increase stability

Cross-section of six-groove rifled bore

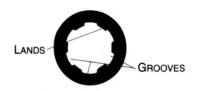

LANDS — GROOVES

RIMLESS—rim of the cartridge is the same diameter as the body

RIMMED—rim is wider than the body of the cartridge

RIMFIRE—a cartridge discharged by a strike to the rim (generally .22 caliber)

RINGS—devices used to support the scope (available in 1″ or 30mm)

ROUND—a term for one complete cartridge

SAFETY—a mechanical device to prevent weapon firing

SAS—Special Air Service

SCOPE—optical sighting device

SCOPE CAPS—dust covers protecting elevation and windage adjustments

SCOPE COVERS—covers to protect scope lenses

SEAL 6—Navy Counter Terrorist Team

SEB—Special Enforcement Bureau (Sheriff)

SEMI-AUTOMATIC—a weapon system that automatically reloads itself but only fires once on each trigger pull

SERT—Special Emergency Response Team

SLING—leather strap used to increase stability while shooting

SO—sniper observer

SOFT POINT—bullet with exposed lead tip designed for increased expansion

SOLVENT—chemical compound to remove fouling from bore

STOCK—wood or fiberglass part of a weapon system designed to support the action and barrel and facilitate shooting

STTU—Specialized Tactical Training Unit

SWAT—Special Weapons And Tactics

SWIVELS—attachment points for sling to stock

TERMINAL BALLISTICS—the study of the effect of a bullet's impact on the target

TERMINAL VELOCITY—speed of the bullet upon impact with the target

TL—team leader

TORQUE—turning force applied to screws or bolts

TRACER—phosphorescent projectile visible at night

TRAJECTORY—the path of a bullet in flight

TRI-POD—three point rifle support

TWIST—the angle of rifling in relation to the axis of the bore measured by length of barrel required to make one full turn (1 turn in 10 inches)

VELOCITY—speed of projectile

WINDAGE—adjustment on scope to compensate for horizontal deflection of bullet

X—power of scope magnification (10X, 3X-9X)

ZERO—setting the sights so point of impact is identical to point of aim

Robar SR-90 300 Winchester Magnum

156

EQUIPMENT SUPPLIERS

SWAT EQUIPMENT:
Eagle Industries, 400 Biltmore Dr, Suite 530, Fenton, MO 63026,
(314)343-7547, FAX(314)349-0321
Tactical Survival Specialties, 1834 S. Main St, Harrisonburg,
VA 22801. (703)434-8974
The P.R.O. Shop, P.O. Box 201451, Austin, Texas 78720
(512)339-1393
Shomer-Tec, P.O. Box 2039, Bellingham, WA 98227
(206)733-6214
K-Zone, P.O. Box 45135, Los Angeles, CA 90045
(310)337-1037
Richard Cowell Co., Box 538, El Dorado, CA 95623
(916)622-8333, FAX (916)626-SWAT
Safety Systems Corp., P.O. Box 2037, Hanover Park, Illinois 60103
(708)653-1103, FAX(708)653-6325

SNIPER RIFLES:
Heckler & Koch, 21480 Pacific Blvd, Stirling, VA 22170-8903
(703)450-1900, FAX(703)450-8160
ROBAR, 21438 N. 7th Avenue, Suite B, Phoenix,AZ 85027
(602)581-2648, FAX (602)582-0059
McMillan Bros. Rifle Company, 21438 N. 7th Avenue, Phoenix,
AZ 85027. (602)582-3713
McMillan Gunworks Inc., 302 West Melinda Lane, Phoenix, AZ 85027
(602)582-9627, FAX(602)582-5178
H-S Precision Inc., 1301 Turbine Dr, Rapid City, SD 57701
(605)341-3006, FAX(605)342-8964
Remington Arms Company, 620 Green Valley Rd, Suite 304,
Greensboro, NC 27408-7725 (919)299-4032, FAX(919)292-3772
Knight's Armament Co., 7750 9th St. SW., Vero Beach, FL 32968
(407)562-5697, FAX(407)569-2955
GSI/Steyr, 108 Morrow Ave, Trussville, AL 35173
Barrett Firearms, P.O.Box 1077, Murfreesboro, TN 37133
(615)896-2938, FAX(615)896-7313
Accuracy International, P.O. Box 81, Portsmouth, Hampshire,
England. PO3 5SJ. (0)705-671225, FAX(0)705-691852
AWC Systems Technology, P.O. Box 41938, Phoenix, AZ 85080-1938
(602)780-1050, FAX(602)780-2967
Precision Imports (Mauser), 5040 Space Center Drive, San
Antonio, TX 78218. (800)662-1980
Sako Ltd., P.O. Box 149, SF-11101 Riihimaki, Finland
(358)14 7431, FAX(358)14 720446

SCOPES & MOUNTS:
Leupold & Stevens, P.O.Box 688, Beaverton, OR 97075
(503)646-9171
McMillan Optical Gunsight Company, 21438 N. 7th Avenue, Phoenix,
AZ 85027. (602)582-3713
Swarovski America, One Wholesale Way, Cranston, RI 02920
(401)946-2220, (800)426-3089
Bausch & Lomb, 9200 Cody, Overland Park, KS 66214
(913)752-3400, (800)423-3537, FAX(913)752-3550
Carl Zeiss, Box 2010, 1015 Commerce St, Petersburg, VA 23803
(800)446-1807, (804)861-0033, FAX(804)862-3734
Kahles USA, P.O. Box 81071, Warwick, RI 02888
(800)752-4537, (401)946-1922, FAX(401)946-2587
Burris Co., 331 East 8th St, Greely, CO 80632
(303)356-1670
California Competition Works, PO Box 4821, Culver City, CA 90232
(310)839-4320
Kowa Inc, 20001 S. Vermont Ave., Torrance, CA 90502
(800)966-5692, (310)327-1913
Premier Reticle, 920 Breckinridge Lane, Winchester, VA 22601
(703)722-0601
Southwestern Firearms, Inc., P.O. Box 69, DeSoto, TX 75123
(214)223-0500, FAX (214)223-9030

STOCKS:
McMillan Fiberglass Stocks, 21421 N. 14th Avenue, Phoenix, AZ 85027
(602)582-9635, FAX(602)581-3825
H-S Precision, 1301 Turbine Drive, Rapid City, SD 57701
(605)341-3006, FAX(605)342-8964

COMMUNICATIONS:
New Eagle (NEC), 201 Railroad St, Silver Lake, KS 66539
(913)582-5823
TEA Inc.,(Lash/Davis) Box 393, South Salem, NY 10590-0393
(914)763-8893, FAX (914)763-9158
Davis Communications, Sutton Rd, Wigginton, York YO3 8RB,
England. (0904)760111, Int.+44-904-760111

NIGHT VISION:
NVEC Company, (VARO), P.O. Box 266, Emmaus, PA 18049
(215)391-9101, FAX(215)391-9220
Litton NVD, 1215 S. 52nd St., Tempe, AZ 85281
(602)968-4471, FAX(602)966-9055
Litton Systems, P.O. Box 429, College Park, MD 20740
(301)454-9904
Aerolog Indust.(NVEC/VARO), 17029 Devonshire St,#151,Northridge,
CA 91325. (818)993-6628, FAX(818)886-0845
ITT Electro-Optical, 7635 Plantation Rd, Roanoke, VA 24019
(703)563-0371, FAX(703)366-9015 *(continued on page 160)*

APPENDIX "C"

ADDITIONAL READING

USMC Sniper Manual

US Army Sniper Training Manual. TC 23-14

Counter Sniper Guide. US Army MTU

M14 and Rifle Marksmanship. US Army FM 23-8

The Tactical Edge by Charles Remsberg, Calibre Press

A Guide to the Development of Special Weapons and Tactics Teams by John A. Kolman, Thomas Publishers

Speer Reloading Manual (or Hornady or Sierra, etc.)

Competition Shooting by A. A. Yur'yev, NRA

The German Sniper 1914-1945 by Peter R. Senich

The British Sniper by Ian Skennerton

Limited War Sniping by Peter R. Senich

The Pictorial History of U.S. Sniping by Peter R. Senich

Delta Force by Col. Charlie A. Beckwith, USA (Ret.) and Donald Knox

also from S.T.T.U.:

SNIPER II—by Mark V. Lonsdale/STTU
RAIDS: A Tactical Guide to High Risk Warrant Service
     —by Mark V. Lonsdale/STTU
ADVANCED WEAPONS TRAINING for Hostage Rescue Teams
     —by Mark V. Lonsdale/STTU
C.Q.B.: A Guide to Unarmed Combat and Close Quarter Shooting
     —by Mark V. Lonsdale/STTU
SRT DIVER: A Guide for Special Response Teams
     —by Mark V. Lonsdale/STTU

Kigre Inc. (SIMRAD), 100 Marshland Rd, Hilton Head, SC 29926
(803)681-5800, FAX(803)681-4559
Star-Tron Tech., 526 alpha Drive, RIDC Industrial Park, Pittsburg,
PA 15238. (412)963-7170, (800)842-7170, FAX(412)963-1552
Meyers & Co, 17525 NE 67th Court, Redmond, WA 98052
(800)327-5648, (206)881-6648
STANO Components, P.O. Box 2048, Carson City, NV 89702
(702)246-5281, FAX(702)246-5211

SHOOTING ACCESSORIES:
Creedmoor Sports, P.O. Box 1040, Oceanside, CA 92051
(800)541-7162
Champions Choice, 223 Space Park South, Nashville, TN 37211
(800)345-7179, (615)834-6666
Champion Shooters Supply, P.O. Box 303, 42 N. High St, New Albany,
OH 43054 (614)855-1603
Gunsmithing Inc, 111 Marvin Drive, Hampton, VA 23666-2636
(800)284-8671, FAX (804)838-8157
Harris Engineering (Bipods), Barlow, KY 42024
(502)334-3633, FAX(502)334-3000

PROTECTIVE FINISHES:
ROBAR(Polymax & NP3), 21438 N. 7th Avenue, Suite B, Phoenix, AZ
85027 (602)581-2648
Birdsong (Black T), P.O. Box 9549, Jackson, MS 39286
(601)366-827G

TACTICAL RIGS:
Eagle Industries, 400 Biltmore Dr, Suite 530, Fenton, MO 63026
(314)343-7547, FAX(314)349-0321
Davis Leather, 3930 Valley Blvd, Unit D, Walnut, CA 91789
(714)598-5620
Safariland, 3120 E. Mission Blvd., Ontario, CA 91761
(714)923-7300—FAX (714) 923-7400
Galco International, 4311 W. Van Buren, Phoenix, AZ 85043
(602)233-0956
Uncle Mikes, 7305 NE Glisen, Portland, OR 97213
(503)255-6890, FAX (503)255-0746
Las Sana, 8960 North Fork Drive, North Ft. Myers, FL 33903
(800)452~5522, FAX(813)995-7125

RAPPELLING SUPPLIES:
CMC, P.O.Box 6602, Santa Barbara, CA 93160
(805)967-5654, (404)235-3426
Columbian Rope Company (fast rope) (601)348-2241
P.O. Box 270, Guntown, MS 38849-0270 (800) 821-4391

APPENDIX "D"

BALLISTIC DATA

The following material was generated using the **Ballistic Data Program** produced by Pro-Ware, Version 2.0.

These particular charts were done on an IBM-PCXT but any home computer could be used to run a similar ballistics program.

The data is based on the Sierra 168-grain Match, BTHP, with a muzzle velocity of 2500 feet per second and a ballistic coefficient of 0.475.

The Key material to note is not the date itself but the **changes** in point of impact caused by changes in altitude, temperature and angle of the shot.

We have used Los Angeles (500 feet) and Denver (almost 6,000 feet) as our example cities and used a cold night (40 degrees F) versus a hot day (90 degrees F). Note that at close range (100 yards) the change in point of impact is minimal.

BALLISTIC TABLE

Cartridge Name-- FEDEAL MATCH 308WIN
Ballistic Coefficient-- 0.475
Alt.-- 500 Ft.   Filename--   SNIPER.308

0 Range Selected-- 100 Yards.
Bullet Weight-- 168.0 Grains.
Temperature-- 40 Degrees F.

Flight Time	Range Yards	Remaining Velocity	Remaining Energy	Total Drop	Bullet Path	Angle +/- 5	Deflection In 10 Mph Wind
0.00	0	2500	2331	0.00	-2.00	-2.00	0.00
0.12	100	2317	2003	2.90	0.00	0.01	0.73
0.26	200	2143	1713	12.34	-4.54	-4.49	3.40
0.40	300	1976	1456	29.30	-16.60	-16.48	7.91
0.56	400	1816	1230	55.04	-37.44	-37.22	14.51
0.74	500	1667	1037	91.88	-69.37	-69.01	24.01
0.92	600	1528	871	140.79	-113.39	-112.83	35.87
1.13	700	1400	731	204.80	-172.49	-171.67	50.80
1.35	800	1288	619	287.32	-250.12	-248.97	69.14
1.59	900	1191	529	390.89	-348.79	-347.22	90.64
1.86	1000	1113	462	519.71	-472.71	-470.63	115.43

Note path of the bullet at an altitude of 500 feet above sea level and a temperature of 40 degrees F.

BALLISTIC TABLE

Cartridge Name-- FEDEAL MATCH 308WIN
Ballistic Coefficient-- 0.4750
Alt.-- 500 Ft.   Filename-- SNIPER.308

0 Range Selected-- 100 Yards.
Bullet Weight-- 168.0 Grains.
Temperature-- 90 Degrees F.

Flight Time	Range Yards	Remaining Velocity	Remaining Energy	Total Drop	Bullet Path	Angle +/- 5	Deflection In 10 Mph Wind
0.00	0	2500	2331	0.00	-2.00	-2.00	0.00
0.12	100	2334	2031	2.88	0.00	0.01	0.64
0.26	200	2174	1763	12.21	-4.45	-4.40	3.06
0.40	300	2020	1522	28.83	-16.19	-16.07	7.08
0.55	400	1873	1308	53.80	-36.27	-36.06	12.92
0.72	500	1734	1121	89.16	-66.75	-66.39	21.31
0.90	600	1603	958	136.21	-108.91	-108.37	32.05
1.10	700	1480	817	196.20	-164.02	-163.24	45.01
1.31	800	1368	698	272.75	-235.69	-234.60	61.04
1.53	900	1269	601	368.27	-326.33	-324.86	80.04
1.78	1000	1183	522	485.83	-439.01	-437.07	102.04

Note less drop at 500 feet when the temperature is 90 degrees F.

163

BALLISTIC TABLE

Cartridge Name-- FEDEAL MATCH 308WIN   0 Range Selected-- 100 Yards.
Ballistic Coefficient-- 0.475   Bullet Weight-- 168.0 Grains.
Alt.-- 6000 Ft.   Filename-- SNIPER.308   Temperature-- 40 Degrees F.

Flight Time	Range Yards	Remaining Velocity	Remaining Energy	Total Drop	Bullet Path	Angle +/- 5	Deflection In 10 Mph Wind
0.00	0	2500	2331	0.00	-2.00	-2.00	0.00
0.12	100	2353	2066	2.86	0.00	0.01	0.52
0.26	200	2212	1825	12.05	-4.33	-4.29	2.64
0.40	300	2076	1607	28.36	-15.78	-15.67	6.20
0.54	400	1944	1409	52.53	-35.09	-34.88	11.19
0.70	500	1817	1232	85.97	-63.67	-63.32	18.10
0.88	600	1698	1075	130.51	-103.34	-102.82	27.32
1.06	700	1584	936	186.97	-154.95	-154.20	38.51
1.25	800	1476	813	256.67	-219.78	-218.76	51.69
1.46	900	1378	708	343.11	-301.37	-299.99	67.62
1.69	1000	1289	620	448.51	-401.91	-400.11	86.23

At 6,000 feet (Denver) the bullet drops even less (40 degrees F).

BALLISTIC TABLE

Cartridge Name-- FEDEAL MATCH 308WIN   0 Range Selected-- 100 Yards.
Ballistic Coefficient-- 0.4750   Bullet Weight-- 168.0 Grains.
Alt.-- 6000 Ft.   Filename--   SNIPER.308   Temperature-- 90 Degrees F.

Flight Time	Range Yards	Remaining Velocity	Remaining Energy	Total Drop	Bullet Path	Angle +/- 5	Deflection In 10 Mph Wind
0.00	0	2500	2331	0.00	-2.00	-2.00	0.00
0.12	100	2367	2089	2.85	0.00	0.01	0.45
0.25	200	2238	1867	11.95	-4.26	-4.21	2.36
0.39	300	2112	1665	28.04	-15.50	-15.39	5.60
0.54	400	1992	1479	51.92	-34.54	-34.33	10.26
0.69	500	1874	1309	84.04	-61.81	-61.47	16.11
0.86	600	1762	1158	126.78	-99.71	-99.20	24.23
1.03	700	1656	1022	181.04	-149.12	-148.40	34.29
1.22	800	1554	901	247.46	-210.70	-209.71	46.05
1.42	900	1458	793	327.87	-286.26	-284.95	59.77
1.63	1000	1370	700	425.79	-379.34	-377.63	76.13

On a hot day (90 degrees F) at 6,000 feet the bullet has very little air resistance.

BALLISTIC TABLE

Cartridge Name-- FEDERAL MATCH 308WIN
Ballistic Coefficient-- 0.4750   0 Range Selected-- 100 Yards.
Alt.-- 500 Ft.   Filename-- SNIPER.308   Bullet Weight-- 168.0 Grains.
                                          Temperature-- 50 Degrees F.

Flight Time	Range Yards	Remaining Velocity	Remaining Energy	Total Drop	Bullet Path	Angle +/- 30	Deflection In 10 Mph Wind
0.00	0	2500	2331	0.00	-2.00	-2.00	0.00
0.12	100	2321	2009	2.90	0.00	0.39	0.71
0.26	200	2149	1723	12.31	-4.52	-2.87	3.33
0.40	300	1985	1470	29.24	-16.55	-12.63	7.77
0.56	400	1828	1247	54.77	-37.18	-29.84	14.16
0.73	500	1682	1055	91.29	-68.81	-56.57	23.43
0.92	600	1544	889	139.82	-112.44	-93.70	35.06
1.12	700	1417	749	202.82	-170.55	-143.37	49.50
1.34	800	1305	635	284.16	-246.98	-208.91	67.39
1.58	900	1207	543	385.80	-343.73	-292.03	88.31
1.84	1000	1127	474	512.18	-465.21	-396.58	112.52

Note the change in the path of the bullet when shooting up or down at a 30-degree angle.

BALLISTIC TABLE

Cartridge Name-- FEDERAL MATCH 308WIN   0 Range Selected-- 100 Yards.
Ballistic Coefficient-- 0.4750   Bullet Weight-- 168.0 Grains.
Alt.-- 500 Ft.   Filename-- SNIPER.308   Temperature-- 50 Degrees F.

Flight Time	Range Yards	Remaining Velocity	Remaining Energy	Total Drop	Bullet Path	Angle +/- 15	Deflection In 10 Mph Wind
0.00	0	2500	2331	0.00	-2.00	-2.00	0.00
0.12	100	2321	2009	2.90	0.00	0.10	0.71
0.26	200	2149	1723	12.31	-4.52	-4.10	3.33
0.40	300	1985	1470	29.24	-16.55	-15.56	7.77
0.56	400	1828	1247	54.77	-37.18	-35.32	14.16
0.73	500	1682	1055	91.29	-68.81	-65.70	23.43
0.92	600	1544	889	139.82	-112.44	-107.68	35.06
1.12	700	1417	749	202.82	-170.55	-163.65	49.50
1.34	800	1305	635	284.16	-246.98	-237.32	67.39
1.58	900	1207	543	385.80	-343.73	-330.61	88.31
1.84	1000	1127	474	512.18	-465.21	-447.80	112.52

Note change in the path of the bullet when shooting up or down at a 15-degree angle.

McMillan M86SR with urban camo stock and 10x-M1 scope.

AWC M29

Wiseman .300 WIN MAG long range rifle with Alpha laminated stock and Ultra 10x-M3A scope.

HK21 scoped for precision shooting.

APPENDIX E

NEW ADDITIONS

Gale McMillan and author at McMillan factory in Phoenix

Robert Barrkman with his SR-60 sniper rifle

Robar long range .300 WIN MAG (top); Robar SR-60 police sniper rifle (bottom).

M-21 SNIPER RIFLE
.308 Cal. (7.62mm NATO)

MODEL 700 BASR
Bolt Action Sniper Rifle, .308 Cal. (7.62mm NATO)

Colt Delta HBAR

Super silenced sniper rifle, SSR Mk 2

Super accurate sniper rifle, SRMk 6

Night scoped, Vaime silenced sniper rifle

French FRF 2.

Model 601 with H-S precision stock (also used on the M-24 sniper rifle)

Mid-Western Mod. 600 .50 caliber

Robar/McMillan .50 cal. complete with Ultra 10x-M1.

Barrett model 82A1 50 cal.

PARKER-HALE M85

Urban camo

Arctic camo

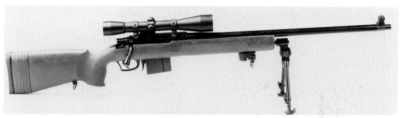

Nato green

Desert camo

Night mode

Fiber Pro stock, model 70 action, Hart barrel and Leupold 10x-M3 scope.

Leupold's Ultra 10x-M3A bullet drop compensating scope.

McMillan M86 with Parker-Hale bi-pod and Ultra 10x-M1 scope.

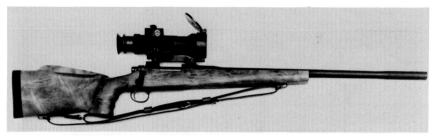

Accuracy Systems' M600 with Litton night scope

FN-FAL with night vision device

Litton M-845 night scope

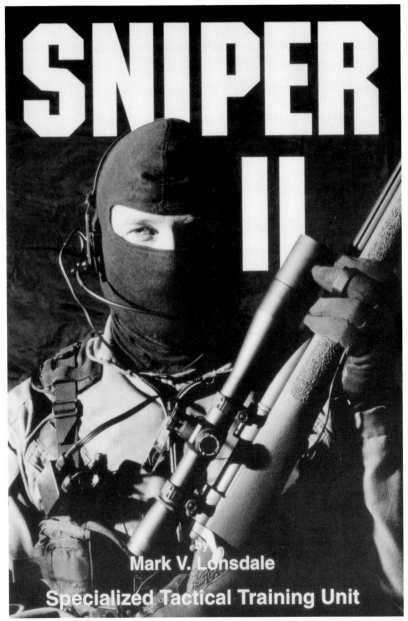